マイ　オウン　ディバイセス

Timeline of Devices

1450-1500 Modern English

Ancient | **Medieval** | **Renaissance** | **Age of Reason**

alphabet **c.1350 BCE**
rotary fan **c.180 CE**
zero **c.600**
rocket **c.1100**
eyeglasses **1285**
movable type **1450**
pistol **1540**
screwdriver **1550**
graphite pencil **1565**
time bomb **1585**
telescope **1609**
multiplication sign **1631**
binary code **1671**
anemometer **1709**
colour printing **1719**
sextant **1757**
electric battery **1770**
metronome **1810**
caffeine **1821**
facsimile machine **1843**

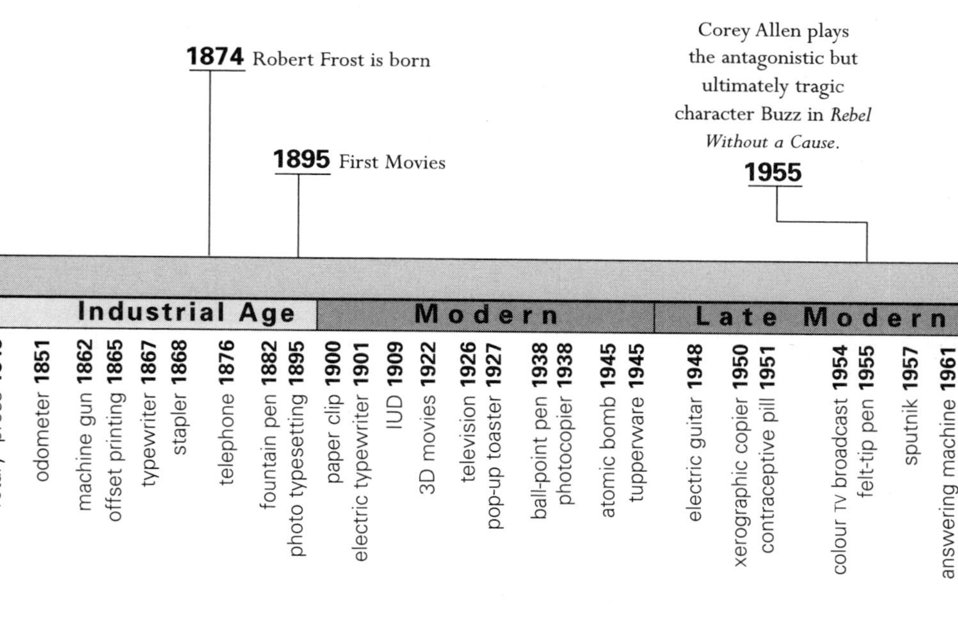

1874 Robert Frost is born
1895 First Movies
Corey Allen plays the antagonistic but ultimately tragic character Buzz in *Rebel Without a Cause*.
1955
Industrial Age
Modern
Late Modern
rotary press 1845
odometer 1851
machine gun 1862
offset printing 1865
typewriter 1867
stapler 1868
telephone 1876
fountain pen 1882
photo typesetting 1895
paper clip 1900
electric typewriter 1901
IUD 1909
3D movies 1922
television 1926
pop-up toaster 1927
ball-point pen 1938
photocopier 1938
atomic bomb 1945
tupperware 1945
electric guitar 1948
xerographic copier 1950
contraceptive pill 1951
colour TV broadcast 1954
felt-tip pen 1955
sputnik 1957
answering machine 1961

1963 Robert Frost dies.

1967 Roland Barthes declares the death of the Author.

1972 July 15, 3:32 PM Charles Jencks declares the end of Modernism.

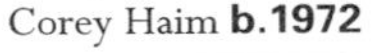

Corey Haim **b.1972**

Corey Feldman **b.1972**

Corey Frost **b.1972**

1972 **1980** **1990** **2001**

P o s t m o d e r n

- quarks **1963**
- BASIC **1964**
- word processor **1965**
- internet **1969**
- bar codes **1970**
- video disk, video game **1972**
- artificial hip, email **1972**
- microcomputer **1973**
- Beta video tape **1975**
- space shuttle **1977**
- neutron bomb **1977**
- Apple **1980**
- artificial heart **1982**
- cell phone **1983**
- CD player **1984**
- CD-ROM **1985**
- Quark XPress **1986**
- inflatable sneakers **1987**
- ecstasy **1988**
- laptop computers **1989**
- inline rollerskates **1990**
- world wide web **1991**
- morphing **1992**
- MD player **1993**
- invisible cola **1994**
- digital pets **1995**
- cloned pets **1996**
- flirt beepers **1997**
- viagra **1998**
- MP3 **1999**
- camera phones **2000**
- passenger bombs **2001**

Corey Frost

マイ　オウン　ディバイセス

MY OWN DEVICES

2002

A flirtation. An auto-iconography. An alibi.

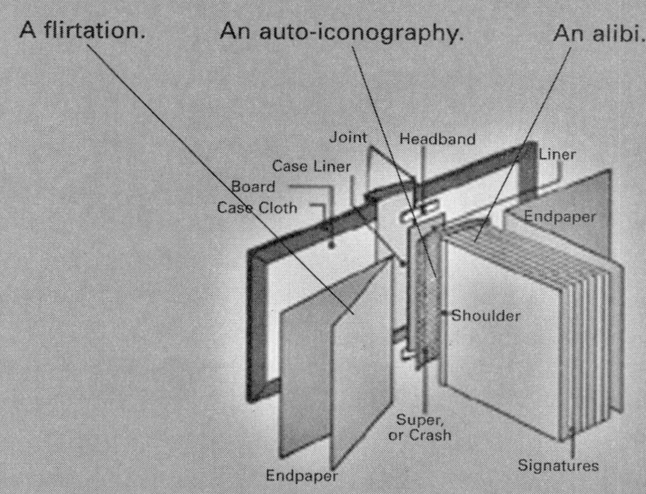

Edited by Andy Brown
Design by Möbius Dick
Cover illustrations (and p. 84) by Marc Bell

Some of these stories have previously appeared in other publications: "Something other than patacas" in *Matrix* 54 (1999). "On opening the door of my mind, I could win love. I also felt affection." in *Slingshot* (1999), and also in the chapbook *Tonight You'll Have a Filthy Dream* (1999), in which also "Blood and gasoline". "Michel Rivard would like to see the sea" in *Headlight* (2000). "A morphology of the Hermitage, by Vladimir Propp" in *Rampike* (2000) and again in the anthology *You and Your Bright Ideas*, edited by Andy Brown and rob mclennan (Véhicule, 2001). "Simultaneous Brazil" as a single-story chapbook (conundrum, 2002).

National Library of Canada Cataloguing in Publication

Frost, Corey
My own devices / Corey Frost.

ISBN 0-9689496-5-7

I. Title.

PS8561.R66M9 2002 C813'.54 C2002-905180-0
PR9199.3.F774M9 2002

Dépot Legal, Bibliothèque nationale du Québec

First Edition

conundrum press
P.O. Box 55003 CSP Fairmount, Montreal, Quebec, H2T 3E2, Canada
conpress@ican.net http://home.ican.net/~conpress

The Canada Council for the Arts | Le Conseil des Arts du Canada

This book was produced with the financial assistance of the Canada Council for the Arts and the Department of Canadian Heritage through IPOLC.

Printed in Québec on recycled paper

A note about the author's name

The name of the author of this work is Corey Frost,[1] which is a real name and not a pseudonym. The results of an informal poll indicate that this is a good name for a writer. Let's examine the reasons why.

Frost, of course, is the name of the famous American poet, Robert Frost, who seriously contemplated suicide. His work is among the most accessible modern writing, given the central theme of all his collections: the quest of the solitary person to make sense of the world. Consultant in Poetry at the Library of Congress starting in 1958, four-time winner of the Pulitzer Prize, Frost is one of the most widely-known poets of the century in the United States: a true poet of the people. The name Frost, however, is relatively uncommon in America and perhaps as a result it has acquired vaguely aristocratic connotations. It has been suggested that this was a factor in Frost's popularity among the working classes. Robert Frost died in 1963. For obvious reasons, it would not be appropriate for a writer to have exactly the same name as such a famous poet — aside from problems of brand confusion and issues of copyright, the name might suffer from a taint of unoriginality. It is, however, effective to capitalize on the prestige of the poet's last name while updating it with the addition of a more contemporary first name.[2]

According to architect and theorist Charles Jencks, 1972 marks the end of modernism and the inauguration of the postmodern era. More precisely, the transition occurred at 3:32 PM, on July 15th of that year, when the Pruitt-Igoe housing development in St.Louis, Missouri, a modernist masterpiece, was dynamited because it was uninhabitable. Corey was a popular name for children born in 1972, which was the year of the author's birth and also the births of Corey Haim and Corey Feldman, who would go on to be teenage film stars of the nineteen-eighties. They would have strangely parallel careers. Corey Feldman was born first, in Reseda, California. Corey Haim was born soon afterwards in Ontario, Canada. Both began their acting careers around the age of eight, at the beginning of the eighties, both eventually winning acclaim in the middle of the decade, Feldman for his role as the easily-excitable Teddy Duchamp in *Stand by Me*, and Haim for the title role in *Lucas*. The story of how they first met, or what agent or producer first had the idea of getting them together, has not been widely documented, but in the late eighties they began to co-star in a number of films, including *The Lost Boys*, *Dream a Little Dream*, and *License to Drive*. Both Coreys seemed to embody the spirit of the eighties teenager, and appealed strongly to that group. However, with the transition to a new decade, and as they both entered their twenties, their appeal waned and their roles became less and less prestigious. Never quite attaining popularity with a wider demographic as did Michael J. Fox or River Phoenix, both Coreys were relegated to low-budget hack comedies, such as 1994's *National Lampoon's Last Resort*, in which they both appeared.

It is difficult to say whether Haim and Feldman's success in the eighties imbued the name Corey with a certain star quality, or whether it was in fact the contemporary currency of the name itself that made the Coreys seem more "cool" to eighties audiences. Corey Hart, a pop singer from Montreal, Quebec, who was also very popular in the mid-to-late eighties, seems to have contributed to or benefitted from the same phenomenon. In any case, the appeal of the name was definitely overspent and wore out quickly. Today the popularity of the name Corey is in decline. The nineties saw a massive decrease in enrollment for the fan clubs of teenage pop stars named Corey. Recent baby name books implore mothers to refrain from naming their sons Brett or Corey.[3] Why the sudden backlash against Corey?

The name Corey seems to connote an immodest optimism that is perhaps too characteristic of the eighties for the tastes of the more world-weary nineties and naughts. It is not a traditionally popular name, hence its appearance in the seventies when there was a growing acceptance of the arrival of societal change. (Note that in the fifties, movie star Corey Allen was not considered to have the star appeal necessary for a lead role, and was cast rather as the villain — for example as the antagonistic yet ultimately tragic Buzz in *Rebel Without a Cause*.[4]) Against the background of the neo-conservative eighties, it would have had the appeal of the safely unusual, along with other trendy names like Jordan, Kirk, Brent, or Alex, without the extravagance of earlier "hippy" names like Rain or Peace. The fact that these names were chosen for their originality by thousands of baby boomer parents at the same time is oppressive evidence of the deterministic omnipotence of demographics. The name Corey, then, is representative of the failure of creativity in the post-psychedelic, media-dominated society of the late twentieth-century, and that is why is it somehow repulsive, while at the same time fatalistically endowed with its own nostalgic kitsch value. Corey symbolizes a generation who were optimistically brought into and brought up in a materialistic world, only to find on reaching adulthood that the optimism had run out.

The author's middle initial is J. The queerness of this letter is exemplified by the fact that in Scrabble™ Brand Crossword Games, there is only one.

Notes

1. When I was eight years old, I begged my mother to buy me blue leotards. I'm versatile and easy-going, and I'm a quick learner.

My Own Devices

2. Stress can lead to the dissipation of mental energies. A pseudonym is only as good as the paper it's written on.

3. If you want to sing out, sing out.

4. That's the edge. That's the end.
Yeah. Certainly is.
You know something, I like you. You know that?
Why do we do this?
You gotta do something. Dontcha?

Crunch! Line 'em up.
You OK?
Yeah gimme some dirt.
Judy? Me too.
Mmm?
Um. May I have some dirt, please?
Hit your lights!
Aaaahhh!
Where's Buzz?
Down there.
Let's get outta here.
Down there. Down there's Buzz!
This is fine.
You be all right?
Judy? You wanna see a monkey?

Hey, you wanna come home with me? I mean, there's nobody home at my house and heck I'm not tired. Are you? You see I don't have too many people I can talk to.

"Quote Quiz"

Jean-François is stymied! He knows that one of the quotes below is the actual epigraph for this book, but he doesn't know which one! Help him find the real epigraph, then turn the page to see how you did!!

The dream: to know a foreign (alien) language and yet not to understand it: to perceive the difference without that difference ever being recuperated by the superficial sociality of discourse, communication or vulgarity. — Roland Barthes, *The Empire of Signs*. 1970

The new means of communication accentuate and strengthen non-communication. — Octavio Paz, *Claude Lévi-Strauss*. 1967

The end of the century is in a sense where we put our history on sale. Modernity is over, the orgy is over, the party is over: everything must go! In the past, the big sales happened before the major holidays. Today, sales are all year round. — Jean Baudrillard. "A l'Ombre du Millénaire ou le Suspens de l'An 2000." 1998

Juggling meta-theory, careful to reveal a touch of polyglot savvy just this subtle side of arrogance, I contradict my paradigm, seeking not effacement of self from Japan, but mastery, power and identity. Authenticity in/by margins, doodled brighter in foreign script. — George Fogarasi, "All That is Soridu Melts into Kitty." 1997

Happy End of the World — Pizzicato Five, album title. 1997
("This record comes with a coupon
that wins you a round-the-world-trip.")

List of illustrations

Their *liaison* began with English lessons. It was early August and the heat made them light-headed and dumb, and words seemed to melt on their tongues like maguro sashimi. This is how he relates it to me, in any case. "Even now, when I think of that first sultry summer," he writes, "I can smell the heady scent of azaleas and hear the incessant hypnotic whirr of the cicadas. [He has a fetish for adjectives.] I still remember her bringing a single white water lily to that first class, and explaining that her name, Hanako, meant flower-child. She was twenty-seven." He didn't realize, at first, where their arrangement would lead, or how painfully it would end, although he admitted that on many humid nights he lay awake on the futon, completely naked but for a thin white sheet, imagining what might happen.

Her friends, Ayumi and Chinatsu, gradually lost interest in the classes, and she came to the apartment by herself after that, on Friday nights because that's when she could leave her office job a bit earlier. She said she preferred conversation to the textbook, and she was too advanced for the book anyway. Their talk revolved around the same things every week: travelling abroad, food, seasonal traditions. One night she confessed how lonely she was. He had just come back from Korea and was talking about *Fusui*, which is what the Japanese call the art of arranging furniture and buildings.

During the occupation, he explained, the Japanese colonial army had built their capitol directly in the path of an imaginary line of power, set out by the rules of *Fusui*, between Kyongbukkong Palace and the govermental buildings. It was a symbolic slap in the face to the Koreans but also it was based on a very real belief that disrupting this ancient balance would leave the kingdom weak and vulnerable. He asked Hanako if *Fusui* was still important in Japan. "I have a friend," she said, "who studied *Fusui* and put her room in the right way to find a husband, and one year later she married a person, and so she told me to try it also."

"Do you want to get married?" he asked.

"Mmm." She tilted her head politely. "Well, I would like to find a boyfriend."

"What do you have to do?"

"Well, if you want to marry you can sleep with your head at the east, and you can put the television and the radio at the south, because the sun gives us... good power. But..."

"But what?"

She laughed a little, but solemnly. "But for me," she said slowly, "it is not working."

Hanako always had a bewildered, hesitant look in her eyes. She was smart and kind: she remembered the most obscure words, like 'sidekick' or 'ecstasy', and yet was constantly awed by the most primitive attempt on his part at learning Japanese. Her face was round with very pink cheeks, and she always wore something feminine and soft, something clingy that would allow him to see the strap of her bra crossing her collarbone, her nipples pressing against the fabric.

She started coming right after work, and they would make dinner. By this time she was teaching as much as she was learning, and she would stay until ten. A few months after the *Fusui* conversation, she brought a bottle of sake and after dinner they sat on the tatami drinking. She spoke wistfully about her friend's wedding, and he abruptly asked what kind of boyfriend she was looking for. Ten o'clock came and she looked at her watch but did not leave. The bottle of sake was finished, and they continued talking about nothing. Around eleven-thirty there was a long

This is a beautification enforcement area.

pause. It was May by then, and getting warm; he was wearing shorts, and she was looking at the hair on his legs. She looked up, very flustered. "I have never touched…" and she reached over and ran her fingers over his knee. He leaned forward and kissed her. She put her fingers through his hair, kissed him frantically, and then started to cry and smile at the same time. He recklessly chose to ignore it.

He told her not to pay for the lessons anymore, but she still came every Friday, and then every Tuesday as well, and they necked on the tatami in the living room, but she always refused to have sex with him or to stay overnight. Through the summer and Fall he grew more and more fond of her, but communication in either of their imperfect second languages was necessarily somewhat shallow. She seemed, to him, to be very happy.

She didn't want other people to know about them, so on weekends they always travelled to other cities and stayed in love hotels together. They never went out together in the town, even to go shopping. In late December, she was planning to go home to Chiba-ken, near Tokyo, for New Year's. He suggested they go together. She smiled and talked excitedly about elaborate plans for introducing him to her parents.

On Christmas Day, two days before the trip, she came over with presents after work, and said she would stay the night for the first time. "I brought some cake. It's Christmas cake, just like me." She smiled mischievously. In Japan, "Christmas cake" can mean an unmarried woman — because common wisdom is that no one wants her after the age of twenty-five.

Later in the evening she said, "Before I introduce you, I think it is good if we are formal. I want you to be direct with me." He asked her what she meant, but immediately realized that she was expecting a proposal. He explained that he had no intention of ever getting married and liked the way things were. She became silent and refused to look at him, said she had better pack some things and left in a hurry. The next day, she phoned to say that she had decided to go to Chiba-ken alone and that she would see him when she got back in a few days.

Two weeks later he got a letter. His hands trembled as he opened it. At this point, the opening titles and the theme music begin to play, as we see a shot from the air of a small car travelling along a highway beside the Japanese Pacific coastline. It is the beginning of a *Japanese Road Movie:*

Moko and Now, after the bubble

I wake up because I hear a sudden beeping, three or four times, which then stops. Behind it there is a windy, whistling noise. Gradually I become aware that my cheeks are freezing, and I realize my face is pressed against something smooth and hard. I'm shivering and confused. I'm in something like a car, obviously. Such a familiar feeling, travelling in a car. You feel it with some unidentified sense; you don't even need to look or listen or smell or taste or touch. I open my eyes, calmly waiting for my memory of reality to return. On the dash in front of me it says "Today" and then in smaller letters, "Humming". Outside, a guard-rail is speeding by. And — this is strange — it's snowing. Before I become fully conscious, this much registers: this car, my car, must be on the expressway. This is my car. But I'm asleep, so who is driving? Panicking momentarily, the way I used to do when passing other cars and looking for the driver's face in the wrong side of the windshield, I sit up and turn to my right, to see who is in the driver's seat. It is no one I know, however. There is a young man there, head shaved except for a Hare-Krishna-type pony-tail on top, cigarette hanging from his red-lipsticked lips, trailing smoke out the edge of the window which is whistling. He doesn't notice that I'm awake. I feel a chill, and then it starts to come back to me.

Hours earlier. The back window of the car passing us is filled with a sea of plush dogs, penguins, and robots, and the dash of the Today Humming is similarly cluttered with Pocky Sticks, Collon, a Nescafé can *ko-hii* for me and cold oolong tea for Moko and Now. Dried jerky for them and dried squid for me 'cause I'm vegetarian. Mentos. UFO noodles: ramen in a plastic saucer.

My Own Devices

There's no CD in the Today Humming, so Moko made a tape: her friends Deathology, Pantera, Red Hot Chili Peppers, and anomalously, the Grateful Dead.

My favourite device is a mini-disc recorder with a tiny digital microphone, which I bought in Osaka, in Den-Den town, which means, roughly, "Electric electrical town". It plugs into the cigarette lighter, and I have the microphone pinned to the Ultraman figurine on the dash, just to collect random bits of conversation: *What is that thing there? / What? / That thing there, what is it? / I don't know. / I see those everywhere. / Oh, I don't know. Maybe… / Is it some kind of code? / Mmm. Yes, maybe some kind of code. Maybe.* This is the improvised dialogue for our road movie.

Tomorrow I will be taking a nap in a train station parking garage near Tokyo, and then I will have to wake up and find my way to Asakusa for New Year's, so I can ring a large bell and watch all of Tokyo eating squid-on-a-stick. It's about ten in the evening of December 30th, Heisei 8, and we're on the Chugoku Expressway, somewhere in Okayama or Hyogo-ken. Twenty-six hours from now we'll be leaving Heisei 8 behind. I'm thinking about how in 1999 everyone in the world — Japan included — will be watching that Times Square clock on TV or the Eiffel Tower, and then the next morning in Hiroshima the calendar will be turned from a routine 11 to an unspectacular Heisei 12. It seems unfitting, especially since Japan will be one of the first countries to be completely engulfed in the new millennium — and sometimes seems engulfed already, in some other millennium. The only way that calendar would roll over to 1 is if the Emperor, suddenly, should happen to die. He must think about this sometimes, when he goes to bed at night. I'm supposed to be seeing the Emperor on the day after New Year's — it's his big day, when he comes out on the balcony with his family to wave hello to a few million assembled mortals. Moko and Now, in the meantime, are going to see their favourite band, Pantera, in concert.

I want to play the recording I made of Loosey Lethe — a name of Moko's own devising, Lethe like the river in Hell — but they won't let me because it's too bad. I recorded them last week, after months of pleading to let me come to the rehearsal. I ran into them in the sock-and-stuffed-animals store at YouMe Town and they invited me along.

A small dream. Just as you requested.

It was the first time I had met Masaki and Yu, the two guys who serve as bassist and guitarist and, for Moko anyway, love interests. She had a thing for Yu for weeks after they met up at K2 studios. One day she told me she was worried because she had confided in Masaki, Yu's friend, and that night she was going to call Masaki to get a report on Yu's feelings toward her. When I saw them next week her pocket bell went off and she excused herself to dig out her cell and make a call. Afterwards I asked her who it was. "My lover," she said. "Yu?" I asked. "No no." She and Now laugh. "Masaki."

In big letters on the wall outside the rehearsal studio, it says, "The purpose of Loft Village is to give people a chance to see into each other's lives and minds." Inside, it's noisy, but Moko and Now and Masaki are sitting down to the usual oolong cha and cup-noodle. Masaki is sort of goofy and shakes my hand vigorously, then he apologizes that he doesn't speak any English. Yu, the guitarist, is alone on the stage pounding away on his glittery blue guitar. It's obvious that as a musician he's the most adept, but unlike Moko he doesn't know how to *be* a rock star. He's too shy, and he doesn't know how to look good in outrageous sunglasses. He comes over with an intense grin and shakes my hand: "*How do you do?*" he says. He's wearing a black Iron Maiden t-shirt.

Moko's in her leather lace-up skirt and an orange and green shirt: it says HELTER. Moko is a paradox. She has shown me pictures of herself on her coming-of-age day, in a kimono that cost half-a-million yen, and pictures of her practising *kitsuke* — the art of dressing people in traditional Japanese garments. (Last year she won the national championship, and since *kitsuke* is rarely practiced competitively in any other countries, we've decided that she can claim the title of world champion.) Her real name is Motoko: a sensible, subdued, feminine name. She appears to live half of her life — the half her mother controls — in some pre-Sony-Walkman, pre-economic bubble, un-disillusioned Japan. But in the half she controls herself, she lives with a preternatural sense of futuristic cool. As if she's already a rock star and is just waiting for the rest of the world to recognize it. This week her hair colour is red, the same colour as the megaphone she's using to sing through, since they apparently couldn't get the mic loud enough. I accidentally press the siren button, but only Now thinks this is funny. Now's name is usually Nao — but she likes to spell it n-o-w like the English word — and she's a part-time hairdresser, as is Moko, in Moko's mother's salon. She is such a beautiful wallflower: bee-stung lips, sunny disposition, slight overbite, obsessed with UFOs — she puts on her glasses so she can read the music. She's the drummer and she's earnest but she can't keep a beat and it doesn't bode well for their muffled and syncopated version of

"Airplane" by the Red Hot Chili Peppers. She knits her brow as she concentrates on the paper in front of her, and meanwhile Moko is yelling at the mic as if addressing a riot. I've never heard the song before, and I don't understand a word.

When we left Hiroshima it was 16:44. The sun had been out all afternoon; there were beads of water sparkling everywhere and a constant dripping sound outside my apartment. In the early morning there had been a snowfall but it had evaporated back into the sky, making it purple. The ticket from the machine at the expressway tollbooth said 16:44, and I stopped the car for a minute to adjust the clock I had glued to the dash, because it was off by several hours. The numbers remained fixed in my head after that — like that wristwatch in the Peace Museum, that is frozen at 8:15 and will be forever. Steam was rising off the pavement as we drove up the ramp to the expressway.

There is hardly anyone on the road because people at this latitude are afraid of snow, but actually the expressway is entirely cleared off — except for some slush in the tunnels and on the mountain passes — so it's great driving weather. When I go over 90 km/h, the speedometer beeps loudly so we boost the volume to drown it out and drive at 100, which is as fast as the Today is capable of humming. It took just two hours to make it from Hiroshima to Tsuyama, our first Service Area stop for Pocky and Coffee. At this hour, we're getting all our nourishment out of vending machines. In Toyota, which is two or three hours away, we're supposed to pick up Moko and Now's friend Death, the leader of Deathology. I haven't met him, but I've seen some snapshots from Moko and Now's last trip to Tokyo — Now has a crush on him, according to Moko. He'll be waiting at the expressway bus stop. Another quick stop for gas and a free half-dozen eggs, then we're back in the orange glow of the expressway.

Now is sitting in the middle of the back seat wearing 3D sunglasses. I keep pretending that I'm a monster in the rear-view mirror and she pretends to be afraid. Moko is getting very tired of this joke and looks out the window, humming along nonsensically to death metal lyrics. I'm not even sure sometimes whether Moko and Now like me, or if they just hang out with me because I'm a *gaijin*. They're not like anyone else I know in Japan and I've always been slightly puzzled as to the nature of our relationship. I think the motivation all round is partly voyeuristic, partly status-seeking. Moko actually said to me once that being seen with a foreigner would make them more cool. I don't know if they realized that knowing them might make me more cool too. The car is beeping.

Moko points out the array of cameras spanning the high-speed road. The cameras are connected to radar and take a snapshot of your car and license plate if you are speeding. You get the ticket in the mail a few days later, along with a picture of the car, you, and whoever happens to be riding in the passenger seat. It has been the cause of many divorces in Japan, Moko says. I ask her how she knows this and she and Now laugh. I very often get the impression that Moko exists in a *demi-monde* of which I have not had even a glimpse, that something is going on that I don't get. I asked her once why she bothers to carry a pocket pager when she has a cell phone, and she just said that she needs it. When she is in Tokyo. And with a conspiratorial glance at Now, she changed the subject. Perhaps, though, all that is going on is language, in its typical impenetrability. Once I went to get my hair cut at the beauty salon where the two of them work, and Moko was clearly mortified when I showed up. The middle-aged woman whose hair she was dying black, on the other hand, was so pleased with my presence that she couldn't sit still, and kept asking questions of "Motoko" that I didn't understand. Moko's answers were terse and non-commital, but the client did not seem to notice, just as she did not seem to notice Moko's purple-streaked hair and deranged eye-shadow. As if in her eyes, Motoko was the model of subservient Japanese femininity.

Poor Now has an allergy of some kind to the dying chemicals, and the longer she works at the salon the more red and cracked the skin on her arms becomes. Both of them want to quit their jobs and move to Tokyo, and I'm not sure why they don't. They are always showing me pictures of people they know there and playing me CDs by death metal bands they have met. "Do you not have enough money to move there?" I ask Now after one of these photo sessions. She lives in a tiny apartment above the beauty salon, and Moko lives next door with her mother. "No," she says. "Yes, but the money is okay..." Moko breaks in: "It's my mother. She does not want me to move. I have to stay in her house, unless..." And at that point they look at each other and smirk. "Unless I become a wife," she finishes, and the two of them laugh, and again I can't tell whether they are serious or joking. This leads, though, to a conversation in which they describe to me, with obvious disdain, the tasteless opulence of the weddings of their cousins and acquaintances. These usually include both a Western and a Japanese ceremony, and Moko is sometimes employed to dress the bride in her Japanese wedding kimono, a complicated and arcanely ritualistic task. Their descriptions of the Western-style part of the wedding, though, suggest a ludicrously schmaltzy scene involving yellow tuxedos, fog machines, and Venetian gondolas lowered from the ceiling on ropes. Moko and Now are beside themselves in their effort to explain all this to me and to express their scorn at the same time.

Around Takarazuka, the expressway starts to get congested and the electronic *kanji* scrolling above us say that the road is basically packed all the way to Kyoto. Apparently there's construction happening. We're going to lose some time. I suggest leaving the expressway and taking the secondary highways, and Moko and Now both look at me, and look at each other, as if I am completely mad. Moko calls Death on her cell to say we'll be late, and Now suggests we play twenty questions.

Are you the world champion of something that you haven't told me about? / What? / Well, Moko is the world kitsuke *champion, and I am the world champion of picking up mints with chopsticks... / Ahh.... / What about you? /* Wakatta! *She is the world champion of... death!* (Ha ha.) */ Death? / Yes! / You are good at dying? / Yes, yes.* Misete! Misete! / Following this exchange, Now closes her eyes and lets her mouth hang open, then she sort of slumps over against the seat.

A tiny twig for the heroine in the town.

Seeing Now smiling at me in the rear-view mirror with her funny glasses reminds me of certain TV commercials. I'm glued to the screen for fifteen seconds, but when the ad is over I can never understand what was being advertised. They usually consist of a single, static shot: for example, a woman standing in a small pond, dressed in a frog costume and balancing a large bowl on her head while she sings off key. Or another one, where an angry-looking man is seen in extreme close-up staring at a grape, which rolls away after ten seconds, causing the man to laugh maniacally. These commercials make me feel as if I have been unwittingly translated into some other world in which everyone's brain contains a module that my brain lacks. I often get a similar sensation around Moko and Now, when they burst into laughter for no reason that I can fathom, or try to explain to me the motivations for their actions.

In a moment of silence, suddenly we hear *Für Elise*, speeded up and as played by doorbells, emanating from someone's pocket. Moko goes into a little hysterical performance as she tries to retrieve her phone, but the moment she answers her manner is suddenly grave and brusque. She says "*hai*" a few times in rapid succession and then hangs up, and says a few words to Now in Japanese. "Who was it?" I ask. "Masaki." I say, "Your lover, you mean," teasing her, because she always calls him that. "No," she answers. And she is poker-faced for a few seconds before she says, with a grin because she knows she is going to shock me, "My... *fiancé*." At first I assume she is joking, but she isn't. She explains to me that she asked him to marry her so that she could move out. She and Now seem to think this is an ingenious plan, brilliant in its simplicity, but I would have been less surprised had she announced she was becoming a nun.

The road is filled with cars, and eventually we're moving at walking speed; there must be a bottle-neck. We've been passing the occasional bright purple back-hoe, and yellow signs that feature cartoons of hard-hat-wearing ducks and frogs and tanukis. *What is it in English, tanuki? / Umm, well in the dictionary it says "raccoon-dog". / Raccoon? What is raccoon?* Moko decides it's the perfect opportunity to change drivers, as we sit in three lanes of traffic on the expressway. So I slip the Today into neutral and pull the handbrake, the two of us get out, she hops over the front and I run around the back. The man in the mini-van behind us stares at me in disbelief. Moko and Now can't stop giggling about this for the next fifteen minutes. They're in a good mood; eventually they consent to let me play the Loosey Lethe recording. Aside from "Airplane", there are some other Chili Pepper covers, a version of "Smells like Teen Spirit", and their one original song, "Wonderland" — music by Yu, English lyrics by Now.

In my head the ground shaking hard
Close the gate against my head
when it bursts it will all fall
you will see it will all be over

when I born you tell me what to do
when I die you tell me what to do to
faster, faster, tell me what to do
faster, faster, tell me how to live

What happens when we all don't come back
What happens when we all don't care
I was taken to the wonderland
Goodbye, Everybody DEAD.
what I'm Saying
You don't want to know.

wake up in middle of the night
under the ground starts to shake
why don't you understand
the pain I feel inside my heart

I remember reading, in the *Asahi Evening News*, and then hearing from everyone for weeks afterwards, about that gate. A fifteen-year-old girl was late for school. The rule was that anyone not inside the school gate at eight-thirty, when the gate was closed, was excluded for the duration of the morning; the teacher whose job it was to close the gate observed this rule zealously. So when the girl, who was notorious for being late, attempted a last-minute dash past the sliding iron gate before it slammed shut, the teacher made no allowances. The gate was closed on time, at exactly eight-thirty. At exactly that moment, though, the girl was between the heavy iron bars of the gate and the concrete gatepost. She died before the ambulance arrived, of massive trauma to the head.

Now has changed her red-and-blue 3D shades for her own glasses, but with a pair of miniature flashlights mounted on the arms. Before long we're through the bottleneck, and then we're flying over the Osaka suburbs on an elevated ribbon of pavement, past Itami airport and through a web of overlapping, intersecting highways. The traffic thins out on the way to Kyoto, and the game of twenty questions winds down as well. Moko is intent on staying between the flickering lines. I tell her to wake me up if I drift off, and we'll take turns driving. The next time I look behind me, Now is leaning against the window, staring quietly at the lights of the pachinko parlours and love hotels gliding by below us, like pictures from the floating world. *Is it electric? / Umm, partly. / Is it big? / Relatively speaking. /* Nani? */ Well, bigger than you but smaller than Japan. / Is it… / Bigger than this car? / No. /* Wakatta!

Later, I wake up because I hear a sudden beeping, three or four times, which then stops. Gradually I become aware that my cheeks are freezing. I'm in something like a car, obviously. I open my eyes, calmly waiting for my memory of reality to return. On the dash in front of me it says "Today", and then in smaller letters, "Humming". That beeping, which I'm sure I heard a moment ago: didn't I learn somewhere (Physics class in high school, maybe) that when bodies travel at speeds greater than 90 km/h they beep? Before I become fully conscious, this much registers: this is my car. So who is driving? I sit up and turn to my right, to see who is in the driver's seat. It is no one I know. That feeling I get from the television ads, the feeling that there's something I should have learned when I was three years old but never did, comes over me again. I can't comprehend why this silent smoking apparition, wearing a green striped polyester shirt with huge lapels, is driving my car. For a moment, as if acknowledging my confusion, he turns to me and smiles a bit, gives a little wave of his right hand. "*Konnichiwa*," he says. Then he puts his finger to his lips to politely indicate that I should be quiet, and directs my gaze into the back seat. I look. There's a jumble of bodies, covered in a blanket. In the light from the moon I can clearly see a pretty Japanese face lying against the seat, eyes closed. A pair of glasses dangle in front of her mouth, with two tiny flashlights dimly illuminating the floor. The smoking man has gone back to watching the road. Slowly, carefully, he takes the cigarette from his mouth and tosses it through the crack in the window, and rolls up the window. Then, suddenly, I understand. The entity at the wheel of my car is Death. Relieved, I go back to sleep.

Simultaneous Brazil

If you care to recall, one day I was going away on a long trip and you stood by the side of the road and started to cry, but what could I do? I have to eat, don't I? In those days I was sleeping as much as I could, whether it was late in the morning in my hammock, or just before lunch or sometimes after lunch, or early in the evening, or in the car on the way to the hospital, or under a tree. Following the advice I had received, I put a lot of extra salt on my eggs. To me it seemed the world was on a slant, and the moon was also on a slant. I've always worried that something like this would happen.

I had a shower, and then lay down by an open window and just drifted off in the breeze. Getting through customs and security was easy. I didn't forget the watermelon; it was on the upper shelf and in the middle of the night it fell off and met the floor with a sudden sodden thump, killing no one. I think it's obvious that the situation is drastically different, now that this has happened. It's just like I've always said. Don't be surprised if a hummingbird suddenly appears at your door. I sent it to give you a kiss.

I really wonder about how I've been spending my time, especially now. At around five I have supper: beans, rice, coconut water, pineapple and watermelon. Yesterday I managed to have some limited conversations. I wanted to buy a pair of sandals, some film, and a hat, but I didn't have any luck. I dozed off and my friends threw me in the swimming pool. On weekdays I sit by myself in the Emergency Room and when people come in I write down their names and ages. My Portuguese is not great and sometimes I have to ask them to spell their names three or four times before I get it right. Just doing my job.

Last night I slept with the ants on the floor. All night long I dreamt about water. Water in buckets, water in hoses, water in waterfalls. I hang out with the patients in intensive care and play backgammon. JoséArmando and I went to church, and hung around with two teenage girls waiting for the disco to start. Apparently the priest is angry because David isn't baptised. When we got back home I lay in my hammock and thought about all the places I will never see again, until I fell asleep. Since what happened, I've been drawing diagrams of first aid procedures.

I went to the market to buy some toilet paper and some wine in a jug. "Put it on my bill," I said. I bought some peanuts and tried to make peanut butter, but it didn't work. I spent some time on the toilet, looking at my new photographs. That night the French class sang "*Bonne Fête*", and I baked a cake. We stayed up, listening to the rain, and drew silhouettes of one another by the light of the oil lantern. I talked to Guy in Portuguese for half an hour and later I found out that Guy doesn't speak Portuguese. The wine was horrible, but what do you expect for two bucks.

Joanne laughed at me as she saw me coming up the street in the rain with pamphlets from the Jehovah's Witnesses. The bathroom at her house is very popular with everyone. The fact is, it rains, on and off, all the time. I had laryngitis, but it took Joanne half an hour to notice. Noaldo won't shut up about the nuclear accident, which nobody is talking about since last week. We are running out of bananas for breakfast. Walking home, I was tired, but I stopped at the milk store and made some photocopies. The funny thing is, I'm not really a melancholy person. Usually, I'm quite chipper.

I wouldn't run a marathon in this heat. I got up on the day before Christmas and burnt my tongue on the coffee. I was the tallest person in the church, by at least a foot. I'm the sickly one today. I had a banana, hoping things would get better, but they only got worse. I spent the entire day defecating and vomiting. They hooked me up to an IV. The nurse asked me what I wanted to eat, but I couldn't make her understand me so I drew a picture on a napkin. What they brought me looked nothing like the picture, though.

Six people showed up for the meeting, and I explained contusions. Where was Canada? Nobody knew where Canada was. The toilet was at the back so I was constantly coming and going through the middle of a bridal reception. That night I slept on a hammock in front of the record-player, listening to accordion music. I thought about cremation vs. burial. Someone called on the telephone and I answered. "*Quem esta falando?*" he asked. "Corey," I said. After a pause he asked again. "*Quem esta falando?*" "Corey." Then he asked me the same question a third time. "Corey!" I said. "*Meu nome e Corey!*"

The children who sell bananas are always following us. One kid was asking for money for his sick mother, so Joanne gave him her ice cream. They asked me to sing a song and I sang "Frosty the Snowman". He was a happy big ol' guy, I told them. He had a corn-cob in his hat and a carrot for a nose and a twinkle in his eye. But in the end he had to go away, and he said he'd be back again one day, but he never came back, I said. It's like the carefree days of childhood, I explained. If something happens to you, you can't make up for lost time. The children brought me a broken flashlight they wanted me to fix. The batteries were dead.

José Armando gave me a Bible and a keychain with a miniature roll of toilet paper on it. We wandered around the bus stop looking for

Cooking by images is the modern way.

the bus, but it wasn't there, so we went to another bus stop. I took some pictures, and then we had shrimp for lunch. I talked briefly with the mayor. I explained how to speak French, and then we talked about astronomy and the Soviet Union. At about eleven-thirty I had an insubstantial hot dog. It was New Year's Eve. At midnight everyone waded into the water and kissed one other. I was supposed to have an anal probe exam the next day, but they moved it.

On the 4th of January I had nothing to do. A man walked up to me and asked me how old I was. He had made a bet with his friend that I was thirty. I bought some bristolboard and lasagna and went home and made mashed potatoes and donuts. Joanne asked me why pea soup is better than mashed potatoes. Anybody can mash potatoes, she said. Certain people are not at all happy about certain events that have been transpiring lately. I sleep uneasily these days, dreaming all the time. When everyone was gone, I planted a fern.

I got up a little late and put on socks. We left early — everyone strolling down the street together — and I bought some deodorant and a pencil. Everyone had a lot of suggestions about how things would have to change from now on. We picked some green and red peppers to eat along the way. I sang a song in the truck but no one noticed. We ran over a chicken for the very first time. When we arrived, there was no water in the waterfall. We tossed our hats and scarves over the cliff, but the wind brought them right back. A girl was sitting on top of one of the tiny mountains, and Noaldo said she had been there a long time.

As soon as we arrived at the nunnery, we started to walk in the opposite direction. We walked all the way through town, past the garbage dump, through the shantytowns, down a long red dirt road, into the interior and the mountains. Finally we arrived at the opal mine. A one-man band was playing. JoséArmando told me I should be less timid and introverted. It made me think of when I was eleven and I was on TV because I was raising pheasants, and how I had been so nervous. I've never been sure about what to do in a situation like this.

I've got a Christmas tree I want to sell. It's in pretty good condition; it was only used a few times and it was never decorated with tinsel. I bought it the day after Christmas for twenty-five dollars, but in light of recent events, I'll let it go for cheap. I didn't want it to come to this, but I have no choice. The population of Brazil is about 200 million people and every night those people go to sleep and they all dream about Brazil at the same time. It's not so bad, really. Finally, something we can all agree on. I'm glad that you're okay. When things like this happen, sometimes it helps to think about a happy moment from your past, if you can. I know it's still early, but I'd like to go to bed now. This is my first day in the Southern hemisphere. I will never, ever find another person exactly like you.

Dear: Corey;

Hi! there! How are you doing?

I have a big news!! On 27. Aug, I saw the UFO!! I was so surprising!! Oh! I'm forgetting. One more big news! Do you know this story? The sun have own mind! Because the sunlight is shinning only the earth. Do you understand what do I want to say? I saw a picture from NASA satellite. There was the earth that was being shoned by the line of sun. I was impressed!! Well, I knew a lot of things. The past, the present, the future, the black world and true Nostradamus… etc. Those wer shocking to me. And little dreadful. But little interesting.

By the way, now you are gone, what did you do, "Miko"?

Please write me and send me the cassette tape!!

I miss you.
Love always, Now.

A morphology of the Hermitage, by Vladimir Propp

In St. Petersburg on the bank of the river Neva there is a building with 2000 rooms. It is called the Hermitage Museum, and I have photographic evidence that seems to suggest that I have been there. There exist maps for the museum, and all the rooms are numbered, but they are not in any order. It is not unusual to arrive at what you thought would be a door and to find it is only a wall and a sign saying "closed". When you go to the Hermitage, you must go with the intention of getting lost. You must have faith not in the artificial structure of the map, but in the whim of your footsteps. You must be a-syntactical, paradigmatic and trans-functional. There is no center and no place to begin; the Hermitage is an unstructured structure. When we read such a structure, what we need is not a map but a morphology.

If I have been there, I have only faint fragments of memories, which could be premonitions for all I know. It is ten after five and I'm still waiting for the golden peacock and the crystal toadstool. In a different beginning, it's ten after ten and I'm looking straight ahead, walking past the guard and hoping he doesn't stop me, search my bag, speak to me. Or it's ten after six and I step out through the western entrance — it's over, they close the enormous doors behind me, and a very soft rain has just ended, dispelling some of the heat. It's ten after midnight and the sun is still lingering oneirically over the Neva, diluted, and the needle-spire of the SS Peter and Paul Cathedral is hyper-real. The light is all messed up.

The photos, which are the only hard evidence of my trip, were developed at the Snappy Snaps in Notting Hill in London, so it says

Excuse me for having kept you waiting.

on the envelope. There are thirty-one of them: there's the equestrian statue of Peter the Great, the teenager who tried to pick my pocket in the Metro, the tour guide standing on top of an apartment building, there's Irina, there's a canal, there's some out-of-focus sidewalk, there's the Winter Palace. And more photos in the museum, somewhat blurry from long exposures without a tripod. There's the Roman sculpture, the Egyptian mummies, Titian, Caravaggio, Raphael, Russia's only Michelangelo, and the Dark Corridor covered in Flemish tapestries, there's Diego Velazquez's *Breakfast,* the Malachite Hall, there's Rembrandt — moving forward in time — there's the Barbizon school, there's Delacroix. There's the inside of my lens cap. There is it again. And again. A complete series of photos that show me only that the way is blocked: whatever happened, I can't see it. And then the images emerge from the darkness again. There's Cezanne. There's Léger. And that's the end of the roll. Something is missing: what happened to the Impressionists? What happened to me? Of course, since I'm not visibly present in any of these photos it's possible that I wasn't there at all — perhaps I took the wrong package of photos, someone else's photos. Perhaps I shouldn't have been in London at all.

But I *have* wanted to go to St. Petersburg for a long time, and I do remember calling Tokyo for that purpose, and the man who answered spoke to me in Japanese with a guttural, narcoleptic accent and I remember thinking at first he was Scottish. I arranged a stop-over, purchased a visa for many American dollars. I gave my credit card number to a hotel by email, so it could have gone anywhere in the world. Who knows, really. I'm trusting in the narrative unity of a postmodern world. But I did want to see the Hermitage; it's the largest art gallery in the world, isn't it? And it is in St. Petersburg. I don't know whether I should explain the origins of the images that exist, or the absence of those that don't. I am suddenly on a quest for the missing Impressionists, and I don't even like Impressionism.

Nevertheless, I find myself at eight in the morning in the waking world of Kansai International Airport. This is a starting point I guess, but it seems I'm going in the wrong direction. My ticket says Moscow, and the tail of the plane says Aeroflot. I see it again on the air-sickness bag — Aeroflot — but this time it has changed subtly, as if I'm perceiving it from a different angle. It starts off with A, as per always, but then it becomes slightly Greek. The R has become a P, the L is a chevron and the F has been replaced by a symbol like infinity pierced by an arrow. It is like an alternate history of the alphabet, if everything had been the same except the Roman Empire.

A movie starts. I check the pocket in front of me and find a white card with the inflight theatre program. At the top it says something in Russian, followed by a number one, and then it says *English: Channel Two.* I put on my earphones. If I adjust the dial on the splintering wooden armrest to number 2, I can hear the movie in English, although the words don't match the characters' mouths. And something else is different. I notice that the word on the air-sickness bag has changed. It now says Aeroflot, but in Roman letters. Curious, I pick up the bag and examine it, looking for some sort of electronic device, a liquid crystal display or something, but it's just paper. Smooth on the outside, waxy on the inside, with small print near the top that says, "Fold away from yourself after use." Even more strange is that the attendants appear different as well. They look friendlier, suddenly. When I turn the knob back to channel 1, the letters change to Cyrillic, and the flight attendants revert to their surly Russian selves. I turn it back and forth several times and watch the alphabet metamorphize. I'm not sure how to interpret this device, but it is already making me slightly nauseous. There is a synopsis of the movie in English: "Magic Hunter The policeman Max successfully to pass the test for professional suitability, resorts to fantastic trick. It pushes him in whirlpool of mysterious events: times, persons vary. Light and darkness, innocence and evil, hunter and hunted: the threads of this fascinating tapestry are drawn together in a riveting outcome that will leave you believing in miracles...." The film is rated brown. Everything is starting to make sense.

Some insidious post-structural travel agency has sent me off into the margins on a monster aeroplane with wooden seats. My quest is not going according to plan. Where is the hero, who is the villain? What am I supposed to do in a whirlpool of mysterious events where times and persons vary? Will I have to resort to fantastic trick?

I should not be surprised to find myself sitting on a bench in front of Kazan Cathedral. There is no photographic record of the intervening time, so it must have been uneventful. The details of how I got here seem to be unimportant, so I sit back and concentrate on learning the Cyrillic alphabet. It's almost midnight, and the sky is a sublime pink. It has recently rained. A woman who looks like she cannot contain her mirth comes walking towards me across the park. Nevsky Prospekt is lined with beautiful Russian women, but she has made mirth her own unique attribute, like a special piece of jewellery. She smiles shyly as she circles the puddles and then sits down on my bench, ostentatiously opening a book on her lap. It's Irina, I know her from the photos: wide picture-window glasses, a school-girl blouse and unruly hair. Her self-conscious grin suggests that she knows what's going to happen, and that I am expected to do something, to react in some way. The fountain in front of us is splashing noisily, like a dream inexplicably filled with water.

Finally, as if at a prompt, she closes her book and cannot help laughing as she asks, "Excuse me what is the time?" I tell her it is midnight. It seems ridiculous, because the sun is absently painting the windows across the street, but it's true and I can't think of an excuse. She nods and keeps smiling. The cover of her book is conspicuous to me now, and when I painstakingly transliterate the five letters of the author's name, I am surprised — surprised and a little unsettled — to find that it says Propp, and the initial B must stand for Vladimir. It seems like heavy-handed symbolism, this choice of reading material. It is too much of a coincidence that she should be reading, at least ostensibly, the book that I bought specifically to read while sitting in this park and then left on the train from… I don't know. In the photo, with the soft blue Baroque architecture in the background, she's holding it on her lap, under her crossed arms: that thin red book with its heavy cover. I'm relieved to have concrete proof of its existence. In this other photo: her demure smile, her miniature glass earring, her sudden laughter, hair over her eyes. From under her bangs, her eyes seem to be delighted by our ridiculous situation — it is still bright, the sun still hasn't gone down, and she is still holding that book, and she is laughing.

I ask if I can see the book she is reading, and she smiles and says yes. I had wanted to read Propp because I don't understand my quest and I thought if anyone could help, he could. Vladimir Propp was a prominent Russian formalist. In his *Morphology*, he defines thirty-one elements of the story in terms of their functions, that is, in terms of what each element accomplishes, regardless of how or by whom: lack, departure, interdiction, violation, reconnaissance, delivery, villainy, complicity, mediation, counteraction, donor function, hero's reaction, provision of a magical agent.... In short, he lays bare the bones of the story and shows us that nothing happens accidentally. Then he assigns schematic symbols to each of these functions and their various permutations, so that different stories can be compared diagramatically. Propp distilled the essential structure of the folktale so well that when he put his grandchildren to bed he only had to rattle off a few functional symbols, say "A9 B5 D7 F1 W*," and they would sigh and go to sleep contentedly. Propp was also the one who first stole the word "morphology" from the linguists, who had already pilfered it from the biologists, who no doubt lifted it from the Greeks. Who knows where the Greeks got all their words from. When I flip through the book's pages, it might as well be all Greek because it is printed in Cyrillic and I only speak Roman.

"I'm reading this book too," I say. She nods vigorously and gestures an offering with her hands. "No, no," I say. "I don't want it; I mean I'm reading the same book." Still smiling, she squints her eyes in confusion. She seems disappointed. "I'm reading another copy. In English," I explain. Smiling, looking at the fountain. I can see the English words churning in her mind. Then she asks, very carefully, "Where do you come from?" She says it like it is some kind of test.

I tell her, glossing over some of the unnecessary complications, and then I ask questions to establish in some rudimentary sense her origins. It is not clear to me exactly where she is from. Not St. Petersburg: I can't determine from her explanation, no matter how many questions I ask, whether she is from Estonia or somewhere near Estonia, or somewhere near here on the way to Estonia. She points off in the direction of the river whenever her words fail her.

"Do you like St. Petersburg?" she asks me.

"Yes. So far." She seems to be waiting for me to say more. "Tomorrow I'm going to the Hermitage," I confess.

She nods in assent. "Yes. I also."

This seems to me an inappropriate response somehow, especially since her laugh is pointedly absent, and I think she has misunderstood me.

"I must go," she says. My mind is racing with her partial utterances that seem to transform the conventional meanings of words, but it seems that the stress is not on the "go," which would indicate an intention to leave, but rather on the "must," which would seem a resigned explanation of why she is going to the Hermitage, albeit a veiled and ominous one. She throws me into further confusion then when she stands up, gives me one more slightly unstable smile, and without saying goodbye walks off into the crowd. I watch her until she disappears amid the New Russians and the tourists, and then I see the book on the bench next to me. Inside the front cover, there is a note in elaborate curving handwriting, which I hadn't noticed before. I put it on the table next to my bed, realizing as I undress and pull down the blind to block out the bright orange sky that I have been awake for twenty-four hours, moving, taking pictures. I feel like I am in a Hardy Boys novel, where the action leads from clue to car chase to confrontation in a continuous, impossibly long day without ever mentioning sleep, food, bathrooms, or any of the other natural needs that healthy young men must satisfy.

When I wake up the next morning it is still light out, and I am well rested and I realize that this is the day when I will finally see *Abraham's Sacrifice of Isaac,* and that famous collection of French paintings. Suddenly, I remember the conversation on the park bench. Her earnest, halting English; her laugh. And how she finally had to go, leaving behind her — the book! I reach for the bedside table. There it is! Right where I left it, with the same gold Cyrillic letters and leather binding. I leap out of bed and go in search of *Breakfast.*

I'm travelling down an enormous staircase, standing immobile, with hundreds of other people. I sense that I am getting close to the Hermitage now, but first I have to go underground, for reasons that are unclear to me but nevertheless make sense. We are descending too quickly to read the walls, but they appear to be filled with ads for Pepsi and Marlborough. The surface where I began is vanishing in the distance and I can not yet see the end, while across from us ephemeral faces look to their origin below and destination above. The steps beneath us move so fast because it is such a long way down, and it is such a long way down because we must distance ourselves from the surface — I'm beginning to understand now — we must find our own depth, penetrate these deep structures. In another photo there is a blue and white stencilled sign whose meaning has become iconic — it says "Citizens! At times of artillery bombardment this side of the street is most dangerous!" — so I understand how this depth was meant to provide protection. At the bottom there is a grandiose Rococo ballroom, chandeliers hanging like crystallized cherry trees, angels and fruit bats staring down from the columns. I walk down marble steps to the dancing platforms of a cavern measureless to man, clutching the book in my hand.

A tattered denizen of the ballroom approaches me. He is wearing Nike sneakers, a blue jean jacket that is too small, and four baseball caps, the visors pointing out in all directions as if he has eyes on the back and the sides of his head. He has a thin, diabolical mustache and never looks directly at me.

This is our final and ultimate plan.

"Do you like basketball?" he demands.

"Sure," I say.

"What is your favourite team?"

"I don't know."

"Chicago Bulls." He says authoritatively. "Michael Jordan. Dennis Rodman. Look." He takes a couple of hats off his head and offers one to me. "Only ten American dollars."

"No thanks." I start to turn away, but he revolves around me like an after-image on my retina.

"Do you like Russian dolls?"

I respond by asking him what time it is. As if I have reminded him of something important, he pulls up his sleeve, revealing numerous digital watches, and asks, "Do you like a watch? Very good watches. Look. This one has a calculator." It sounds like he is trying to swallow the beginning of the word calculator. All the watches seem to be displaying a different time. "Do you like? Rubles, okay." I tell him no thanks.

He stands there beside me, not speaking, for a few minutes — seeming bored, I think, or abject. The train comes. As I step through the double doors amid the crowd I realize he is right behind me and he stands next to me as we shudder noisily out of the station. I keep one hand on my bag and hold on to the post with the other, which is also clutching the book. When my interlocutor looks up and sees the cover of the book, his eyes open in amazement. Pointing a finger, he turns to me with silent interrogation. I don't say anything.

"Do you read this book?" he shouts.

I nod my head, and then change my mind and shake it.

"Do you speak Russian?"

I shake my head again, at which he begins digging frantically in his pockets and pulls out a wrinkled and scruffy little book and shows it to me. It is a Berlitz *Russian for Travellers*. He opens it and reads to me to demonstrate how it works. "*Ya nye gavaryu pa Russki*. I don't speak Russian." He laughs loudly and I nod and smile. He flips through again. "*Gdyeh... tsirk?* Where is the... circus? ha ha ha."

He raises his eyebrows and nods conspiratorially with me. "Yes? Do you like? We trade, yes?" and he reaches out his rough, Timex-covered hand towards Irina's book. Without thinking, I abruptly pull the book away, clutch it to me, and I give him a shove with my other hand. I'm surprised by my own belligerence. He glares at me, thwarted, sullen. The train stops and he steps off, still fixing me with his eyes.

I realize when the train moves again that I should have stepped off at Gostiny Dvor also, and I end up surfacing again at Vasileostrovskaya. I will have to walk back across the river from Vasilevsky Island — I am already a bit lost, and I have not even arrived at the Hermitage yet. I wander around the streets, mumbling to myself, "Where is the circus?" But soon I come to the river, and I see it for the first time: the green walls and white Rococo ornaments of the Winter Palace, its gold-capitalled columns lined up along the river like an army of ghosts, and beyond that the Little Hermitage, the Large Hermitage, the

Hermitage Theatre. It looks just as it does in my photos. The castle where the czars lived until there were no more czars. The Winter Palace alone has over a thousand rooms. Now that I'm here, I am a bit nervous about discovering what those unexposed photos did not allow me to see. The encounter with the Timex man in the subway has unsettled me. Something is going on that I don't know about. I sit down on the edge of the Dvortsovy bridge and open Vladimir. I can't remember much about his morphology, and the text is now opaque to me. But I can remember some of the Cyrillic letters, and some are the same as Roman symbols, and with this scant knowledge I try to decipher the print. In Japanese there is a syllabary, called *katakana*, that is used exclusively for foreign languages. Many signs and menus in Japan, which at first appear to be in Japanese, are actually in English if you are able to transliterate the writing. I met children, in fact, who believed that they could make me understand Japanese by writing it down in *katakana*, since that is how you write foreign languages. Maybe in the back of my mind I am thinking about this and that's why it happens. The first couple of words contain a funny backwards three and a little box with legs, but when I figure out the sounds I realize that they say "the word". I go on to decipher the next one: it is "morphology". "The word 'Morphology'." I scan the next few lines and realize that they are all in English. The whole book is written in Cyrillic English. At first a few unfamiliar symbols appear, but it is easy to figure them out, cryptogram-style. It only takes a few minutes of practice before my eyes can translate the letters for me. I'm reminded of those stereograms in malls; they look like random patterns at first, but as you stare at them they slowly reveal a picture underneath.

I am confused by my ability to read, but at the same time relieved because now I can consult Mr. Propp about my quest, ask him what kind of tale this is, what I am supposed to do next and how it will all end up. If I can make sense of the linear structure maybe I can glimpse the paradigmatic, latent content beneath. Reading slowly and deliberately, like a child, I go through Propp's list of thirty-one functions. As I read the descriptions they begin to sound familiar. Lack: the hero realizes a lack of something. Departure: the hero leaves home. Interrogation: the hero is tested, interrogated, attacked, etc., which prepares the way for his receiving a magical agent from a donor. Reaction: the hero reacts to the actions of the donor. Receipt of a magical agent: the hero acquires a helper or magical object. The villain attempts to substitute or take away the magical agent.

I realize of course that Propp is describing exactly what has happened to me so far. I am troubled that he has made me the hero. First, there are the missing Impressionists. Then, I leave Japan on a quest. Next, Irina approaches me in the park, and asks me what time it is. I tell her. As a reward, Irina leaves the book behind, which the Timex man then attempts to take from me. The book is the agent. And inexplicably, I can read it.

Just then I remember the note on the inside cover. The handwriting is so extravagant, though, that it seems almost indecipherable. I have considerable trouble with the first letter, and almost give up, but it is possibly a K. The next letter is an O, followed by a P, which is actually the Cyrillic symbol for R, and then a sort of backwards N which I have learned represents the sound "ee". When I figure this out, I am startled once again, because it spells out my name.

Corey, I am very glad I met you in the park. It was lucky accident. But, I could not understand everything. Some words about myself: I'm interested in a foreign language. I like reading, and looking at paintings. I think it will be very interesting and useful to see you again. Don't be late. I will be looking at a room. It is called Impressionism.

On opening the door of my mind, I could win love. I also felt affection.

The other day I opened the door of my mind, and everything could be seen beautiful. *Women's history never cease to yearn for beauty*, I thought. *I have bought some really nice things. All of my dreams are coming true, also.*

I stop for a coffee after doing some grocery shopping, and then I walk back home across the bridge. It is snowing like a kamikaze. *Kaze*, wind. *Kami*, god. This morning I woke up and it was around 0° in the bedroom, and the heater had run out of kerosene. I had to go to work and I thought I would have a shower, but the pipes had frozen and the water heater wouldn't fire. So I tucked my clothes under the *kotatsu* to warm them up and then went out in the snow in search of kerosene. "*O ko-hii, kudasai*," I say to my friend at the "World Coffee Specialty Shop". He's got an extensive apparatus behind the counter.

Last night, I tell him, I drove home in my car, the name of which is "Windy". As I left the city the line of cars ahead of me was travelling at around 20 km/hour. The snow was barely perceptible. The road is a narrow path too windy to pass, so I drove along in second gear. Amazed at the snow paranoia. But this morning as I walked over the Asahi river, brown and reedy at the edges, the sky completely white and gone, I noticed the blue jump-suited high school students playing soccer in the snow. I don't know what to think about the lack of insulation in the houses. I say all this but my friend doesn't understand English. I drink my *ko-hii*. He just likes having me here.

I'm sick, yes. It wasn't really wintery when I left for Indonesia, but I've had a head that feels jammed full of tangled *kanji* ever since I got back. American natives succumbed by the millions to imported European diseases, and Dutch sailors in Batavia couldn't seem to handle malaria, and I've been three weeks with a Singaporean air-conditioning cold, lodged in the nose of a nordic Caucasian in Japan. A sino-nipponese sinus thing. It is considered very rude to blow one's nose in public. *Nipless*, says the little pink package of nipple stickers that we saw in the airport. *Please put this on your breasts.*

My back wheel falls in the gutter as I try to leave our lane that evening and Tsuboi and his son and his son's friend lift the car out — it is not heavy — and they provide me with admonishments, repeating the words for snow and dangerous. They ignore my grunted and mimed pushing and lifting instructions. I have come to Japan in the hope that I, too, could be misunderstood and subjugated. These men are real, and I am a German art-film dream of an angel in this white yuki — on opening the door, everything could be seen except my long black coat. I stand invisible in the library, having no words for reference. I go to see my friend and ask him for a World Coffee Specialty.

If a young man wants to get along, he should keep his friends strong. *However.* Use this advice whatever you like: there will always be affection between young men who dream together. *Sir, please enjoy yourself with this new-found love.*

Something other than patacas

Moshi moshi. Ano... sumimasen kedo mou nihongo o hanashimasen ga... zero-hachi-roku-nana-yon-ni-go-nana-san-san desu. Sorry we have either gone to Hong Kong or home. So, please leave a message and we'll get back to you BEEP...

Hi.

Umm. It's me. I'm in Macau. Well, in the end I decided not to stay in Hong Kong tonight. It was raining, and I can see on the TV that it's still raining there, so I got on the ferry this afternoon and came here. There were too many drunk ex-pats and tourists running around wearing commemorative t-shirts, and the idea of being crammed in a sweaty crowd of them, in a parking lot in the rain, was, in the end, not appealing to me. I'm working on that article I told you about, and I'm going back tomorrow. I guess you're gone already, so you won't get this anyway. So. There's some kind of wind blowing down the river, now, so the humidity has lifted a bit. I'm doing strange things tonight. Things I wouldn't normally sanction, really. I guess I'm doing some weird things. I had crocodile for dinner. I'm going to the casino, or else the dog races. It's a weird place, this city. It's... I'm having fun but I miss you. I was going to... I'd rather be telling you this, though. Well, that's all.

My Own Devices

June 30, 1997. No one will take your patacas in Hong Kong unless you don't want anything in return, so I have to get rid of them while I'm here, because I want something in return. In returning, I would like to have something more than patacas. I'm going to ask for a winning dog, that I have an urge to trust: I Love You.

Angelo Badalamenti's lonely theme. Crocodile à la Meunière. It was not a bizarre and illicit delicacy of a dinner party in the Forbidden City. It was more like Cap'n Highliner's frozen Tempura Crocodile fillets, with coleslaw and French fries on the side. It wasn't the Jade Restaurant and Opium Den in Macau on the Pearl river, it was more Jade's Diner and Truck Stop on Highway 81.

Since we spent the previous week watching every episode of both seasons of *Twin Peaks* with Japanese subtitles, my overall disposition toward the world in general has been upbeat but hauntingly sentimental. I am dogged by a feeling that I have become a boy magician, I live in a trailer park with my incorporeal grandmother, igniting flames in the palm of my hand. And at ordained moments, sitting in front of soggy cabbage in crocodile grease for example, I murmur cryptically: *J'ai un âme solitaire.* Because everything sinister and true is spoken in another language, or backwards.

Cymbals hissing the card shark theme. The dogs are running tonight at the Canidrome. I eat fish, but never fowl. I certainly never eat cows, but what are reptiles: neither fish nor fowl. Something other. I'm acting like someone I don't know but who will someday through some random action alter my life irrevocably. Talking on the phone with you, to whom I am married, I suggested that I might bring back the experience of money for sex. I often have sex, and I often use money, but what is money for sex? Something other. Sex, I understand, is like international travel. If you haven't done it, it seems like an inaccesible fantasy. But once you have experienced it, you grow gradually more disillusioned as time, countries, and lovers go by.

> the displacement of trade by tourism as an economic *raison d'être*. Some 75% of the state's revenue now comes from gambling and its associated industry — casinos, hotels, racetracks, some built on reclaimed land that has in the past year increased the total land area of the country by a fifth.

Instead I end up in a breathtaking hovel where the floors are worn almost through and the bed is too short, masturbating very quietly because the cells are only divided by chicken wire along the top.

> the people of Macau may find themselves in an even more precarious position. As the present hand-over of Hong Kong was approaching, Portugal was growing increasingly eager to also unload its awkward colonial anachronisms, the result being that scarce provision for cultural protection was made in the Sino-Portuguese agreement that mandates the hand-over of the protectorate in 2003.

The dogs are on a little jaundiced TV screen at the betting center, next to the casino. I put my 500 Macau patacas on the last dog in race number nine, whose name is I Love You. And now, I'm at the Canidrome, where they've just sent a dirty bunny hurtling around the track, as a warm-up for the bunny. Quite plainly it's a bunny, couldn't be called a rabbit. It's floppy, with a bulbous tail, and runs about a foot off the ground. I think of a regurgitated bunny in an Argentinian short story. Everything at the track seems strangely realistic. Men in white suits look like cricket players. The hounds loping along beside them are lean and can only be seen side-on. The hounds disappear when looked at head-on, except for a panting Cheshire tongue. Tails curled up at the end like cheetah's tails, like things that have to run. Simply walking seems painful. Being slow is painful.

> while Hong Kong's airport project is stalled over debate about China's liability for costs, the brand new Macau International airport is a paragon of co-operation between chaotic mother country and its level-headed colonized extremity.

Cantonese announcements. I'm in the bleachers with my Hello Kitty notebook, trying to look serious since all around me are devout men and women dressed in their best Levi's. But I'm not comparing the greyhound schedules, I'm colourizing this article that hopes to go in some far-east economic review, perhaps next to all the glossy pictures of fireworks over Kowloon: the story of "the other colony". A sidebar, perhaps. How does the city look from here? Will we be able to see the fireworks? The most expensive display of fireworks, they say, since the Chinese invented fireworks. A small, but ostentatious, artificial war going on over there. I realize that when I return tomorrow, I will not be returning to the same place. From now on, when I say the name Hong Kong, it won't mean the same thing.

> speaking a dialect of Cantonese distances them yet another step from the standard Mandarin, and a unique Portuguese-influenced cuisine, architecture,

> and other such mundane and malleable clues to identity make the Macanese ambivalent about cultural alliances. they seem to be inflicted with a syndrome peculiar to unwillingly liberated colonies, a kind of schizophrenia manifested in a frenzy of economic revitalization and a fatalism that at the same time induces a massive financial and demographic exodus. Where is the joy, after all, in being folded back into the arms of China so that the colonized can relinquish the economic power that they wield over neighbours who have been liberated from economic hierarchy by communism?

Officially the betting takes place only at the off-track betting centers, but wads of Hong Kong dollars, Macau patacas, and Japanese yen are circulating as what appear to be random gifts among the crowd. I'm surprised to see so many people at the track, most of the city having evacuated to the party across the bay. The faithful remain. One of the greyhounds, wearing purple, is walking sideways.

How much is that dog. I have arrived at race four. Distance: 595 yards. Official condition of the track: good. Next to the bleachers a wooden board displays the names of the dogs and the Chinese ideograms are beautiful but even more beautiful are the English twins. There are seven dogs: Heart Large, Always Victory, Korong Lass, Amerigo Wind, Treasurefull House, Successful Way, and My Treasure. In Chinese, Heart Large is a stick person and a graceful sweep that looks like snake bites in the sky, very high and far away. I recognize the Chinese character that means wind in Amerigo Wind's name: it looks like the insect character inside the house character, minus the person character who is usually inside the house character. I imagine translation as a thrilling, dangerous stunt.

All the dogs are boys, I think, so Korong Lass is presumably not a lass, or we may presume that Korong Lass wants to be. Korong Lass, walking sideways, is now jumping around on the track like a fish. He gets away from his leash and jumps around, way off the ground, but doesn't go anywhere, but jumps and twists around. He is trying to tell us something — I'm running down to the edge of the track, I'm shouting, what is it, Lass? What is it? Is someone in trouble? Finally, tidy white cricket men subdue him and he is led toward a row of small metal boxes and put into one. All of the dogs are put in metal boxes, all in a row. Then the bunny is electrified and starts speeding around the track. As the bunny passes, the hutch doors fly open and the dogs are off.

Stress can lead to the dissipation of mental energies.

The dogs have the ability to slow down time around them, and as a result the dogs seem to be able to run very fast. Always Victory is leading all the way, but is overtaken by Korong Lass. Nobody catches the bunny. After they pass the finish, a white curtain goes across the track and the dogs don't know what to do. The dogs stumble over each other, ecstatically looking for the bunny. Or something other. Whether to feel relieved for the bunny or sorry for the dogs, the frustrated dogs. For Korong Lass, who is led away on a leash, and who, at the end of a short racing career in which she wins many races and lots of money for her owner, will be ejected from a truck onto a barren road in Guangdong province.

> of course, this tiny city-state has little choice but to co-operate, having nothing much on the bargaining table to compare to Hong Kong's moneyed strength. Macau is in the ironic position of fearing that China will close off the land border on which it depends, while simultaneously fearing the fast approaching day when the opposite will happen and the border will no longer be there.

Back at my seat, a man waving dollars and laughing says something excitedly to me. I ask him in Portuguese if he speaks Portuguese. He looks at me quizzically. "No. No Portuguese," he says. "Don't understand Portuguese." I ignore the linguistic illogic of his English response and ask him who his favourite is for race 5. He leans over to me solemnly and says, very distinctly in my left ear, "Wild Phallus." I'm not sure if he understood me, or if I am being insulted, or complimented.

The organ is not played during the race, or, in the excitement, we ignore it. But in the next race is Wild Phallus along with Good Way, Gold Fortune, Chips, Top Hound, Typhoon 8, Enjoy Again, and Foretop. Wild Phallus seems a shoe-in with odds of two to seven. But at the end, while they are rolling around orgiastically in the white curtain, a photo finish reveals that Top Hound has come out on top. I carefully make notes. A new set of names is carried out and slid into place on the board for race six. 475 yards. Eight dogs: BoBo, Breeze 9, Heart Large 2, Good Chosen, All Turbo, Strength Boy, and Miss Bungo, another t.g. runner. And finally, a dog named I Want to Win who looks like he does, prancing down the track ostentatiously. Miss Bungo is pretty and shy with a sleek grey coat.

I turn to the now morose Wild Phallus man and ask him who translates the names into English. I wonder if he could translate me also into his weird grammatical world. I don't expect Wild Phallus to respond but he says it's Mr. Wang downstairs, who paints the signs. Wild Phallus abruptly stands up, and beckons for me to follow him, for I am to meet Mr. Wang. He takes me down the end of the bleachers, around a corner, and through a door into a dark garage where some guys are sitting on chairs smoking.

Mr. Wang turns out to be a man about my age with a big grin and he shakes my hand and says, "Hello, what can I do to you?" What I would really like him to do to me, of course, is to squint his eyes at me and to see in my own eyes dark commas of ink like the ones in the names on his signs, and to write me in what he thinks is my own language. I want him to translate me into something that is supposed to be the same thing but is really something other than equivalent. I say I can read some Chinese, which is not entirely untrue since I learned kanji in Japan. I can tell what many characters mean even though I have no idea what they say. That is, I can read Chinese not as Chinese but as what I think is my own language. Mr. Wang snorts and does not seem barely credulous when I fail to pronounce any of the dog's names in Cantonese. He goes back to playing *mah-jongg* with his friends.

Really, then, what happens didn't actually happen that night at the races, but later, lying rigid on my wooden bed under the chicken wire and white unshaded bulb, I thought of it.

The ancient owner's radio in the Hospedaria Vong Hong, 45 or 253 Rua das Lorchas. Both numbers are on the building. Which is it? Walking back, midnight came, and I didn't see any fireworks. And I took out some paper and started writing this letter to you, telling you why I am suddenly afraid of being ejected from the back of a truck in Guangdong or similarly discarded when I can no longer live up to the name I Wanna Win, when I no longer have a name like snakes in the wind. What I imagined was that Mr. Wang and I became good friends, I complimented his ability to evoke complex emotions in dog names, and he offered me a cigarette. Over there, I said, we have a saying, "to have a smoke." Good day, good smoking. Please, take together, he said. This is the most comfortable smoke I have ever run into, I said. He said the best quality goods always make you happy. They were Lark cigarettes from Japan, and after a thoughtful moment's pause he added, Speak Lark. So I spoke it to him, of how much I hated talking to you on the phone and how I wanted to roll around in the dirt as if we wanted a bunny. I told him that I wanted to leave here with something more than patacas, something they would gladly take in Hong Kong, but I won't give it to them. I told him I didn't know what to say on the phone and that I envied his unremitting eloquence. I told him that I was beginning to believe that if I ever wanted to write beautiful English I would have to completely forget how to speak it, and I don't know how to do that. He smiled and took a drag of his smoke, nodding acknowledgment or agreement. I like you, little bear, he said to me. We had become quite familiar with one another. I was puzzled by that comment but I gave his hair an affectionate tousle. I had taken to calling him Max.

That night Max and I named the dogs of race nine together, putting our whole lives and everything we knew into the work. If I had no idea what the dog's name really meant I translated anyway and felt empowered, made certain, by an overwhelming uncertainty. I started by translating the name of one dog as The Owls Are Not What They Seem, in honour of the unpredictability and mystery of the evening. He loved that, and responded by calling the next one Lucky Accident. I was ecstatically happy that he knew the importance of what he was doing, the importance of naming.

Like a single unified Adam, handing out names to the animals, we could have been the only man on Earth. I called the next one The Effect that Language Has on Perception, and I liked the idea of that concept on the track, racing along with other ideas and beliefs in earnest competition. He named one My Chinese Word and seemed pleased with the paradox. And I called the next one The Effect that Language Has on Events, and on Emotion. Then in my excitement I also named the next dog, calling him Where Is the Joy, After All, in Being Folded Back into the Arms of China So that the Colonized Can Relinquish the Economic Power They Wield over Neighbours Who Have Been Liberated from Economic Hierarchy by Communism? At this point he became very pensive and when he finally did speak again he held out his hands as if offering something and said, "I was very young. Six years old. A girl in my town, we ran up a hill. On the top we can see all the mountains, and rivers. I am very happy, and very not breathing, and the girl also, and I was very exciting that day." And that was the name he gave to dog number seven. I felt that we had achieved something together, something maybe that I could take with me instead of patacas. Finally there was one remaining dog who would be running in race nine. His name in Chinese looked like snake bite ribbons on the ankles of an androgynous runner. It was the dog I had bet on, I Love You. He was the last dog, and the odds were not in his favour but I bet on him anyway. I gave Max a hug.

> and now, 440 years later, the political climate seems to dictate that this speck of Cathay will go the way Hong Kong is going, but the people of Macau may find themselves in an even more precarious position.

Radio off. In the end, as I lie naked in the chicken-wire dark, too leery of fleas and spiders to pull the sheet over my legs, while across the bay Hong Kong is being translated itself, the story of this letter is about dogs: how they fly and how they lovingly wrestle one another in the dirt and how eventually they become bony and sad. I could have given them any of those names or created in them the memory of anything in my life, or any sentiment that floats in between words that I know and words that I don't know. And I would have been happy no matter who won, except that one of them carried with him my only chance of winning too. In reality of course those dogs are just dogs, because they have no foreboding, no premonition of the back of that truck and that lonely stretch of road. They just run and love doing it, and love each other for doing it. In reality Mr. Wang and his assistant carried the dogs' names out on planks like dead bodies. And in reality I watched race number nine, the last race, alone, from the edge of the track where there was nothing between me and the dogs, where everyone in the bleachers would see my majestic triumph or my abject disappointment.

I Love You was near the front for almost half a lap, eyes glowing at the bunny that seemed playful, almost laughing, and my heart was large, and growing larger. But he fell behind, and slightly more ruthless dogs pulled ahead, and then in the confusion of those straining hounds rabid for a bunny, I Love You got jumbled, and stumbled, and then he tumbled and rolled through the dirt like a grub wound in a ball. He got back to his feet immediately and kept running, this time chasing not the bunny but the distant heels of the other dogs, because I Love You is not a dog that gives up easily, or stays down. But he never caught up. I Love You came pounding across the finish line well behind the winners and even the losers too, in absolute desolation, unnoticed by the audience, insignificant, sad, and even slightly pathetic. But he is the one that I bet on, the one that I got instead of my patacas, and he is the one I'm telling you about.

WORD LADDERS!

Changing only one letter at a time, can you transform the word on the first rung into the word on the last rung? The first one has been done for you!

device	**art**	**plane**	**photo**
devise	ark	place	____
demise	____	____	____
remise	____	____	____
remiss	____	____	phone
remits	**irk**	**crock**	**prone**

travel	**bride**	**laser**	**novel**
____	____	loser	____
____	____	____	____
____	____	____	____
____	____	____	____
tropes	**traps**	**dopes**	**rapes**

print	**books**	**ironys**	**words**
____	cooks	____	____
____	corcks	____	____
____	corky	____	____
____	corny	____	____
____	____	____	____
shits	**horny**	**drivel**	**tired**

1996 Rehabilitated

December 31, 1996. 6:30 PM. The Last Resort. *The last day of the year, and my last destination: Bukit Lawang. A tiny village, little more than a path lined with guesthouses along the Bohorok river. An oasis surrounded by jungle. I hoped it would provide a semi-satisfying conclusion to this year. A chance to meet other foreigners at the Orangutan Rehabilitation Center and practice my English, so to speak, since the year will not seem real to me until I have told the story to someone else.*

The ants are coming to visit me because I am on the verge of tears. Here they come, racing and bumbling over each other. So tiny and funny and horrifying. One of them tries to carry off my mug of sweet ginger tea, but cannot bring himself to climb its glass face because it is too hot. I am weak with hunger and I do not know if I will have the strength to fight off the marauders when my tempeh arrives. The ragged line of bumble-ants extends backwards across the table-top and along the edge of the balcony, down the leg of the building and under the grass in the clearing, clear into the huge feather-duster trees along the path. The trees themselves are vague, amorphous entities, blending into one another like molten emerald. Maybe it's my naked eye that melts them, my glasses being at the bottom of the Bohorok river now. Maybe they are just like that. This jungle-wood chair and table are writhing with creepers stolen from the jungle, and in fact the whole jungle is coming to visit me. This is the dead center of Sumatra. It feels like a sand-pit with an ant-lion at the center, buried except for the mandibles, waiting for a hapless ant-elope to fall down the slope.

Something, which I still feel lingering around me, made me

plunge my head into a fast, cold, tropical mountain river while my glasses were still on my face. My glasses that were made in Montreal, whose frames I found in the pocket of a jacket at a second-hand store. They were exactly what I had looked for since my first glasses at age ten — thin silver ovals with long straight arms that stuck out behind my ears — and they had made me feel, whenever I put them on, that I was *happy in my skin*. I am near-sighted, so I can still see this page perfectly well, but my vision of things far off is sacrificed. It comes from many nights of forbidden reading under the covers in the dark when I was young. I cannot see very far. The future, as I know it now, seems to abruptly end at some quickly approaching and strangely familiar moment.

Even as I braced my feet against a rock and lowered my sweaty torso into the current, I had visions of my glasses tumbling away. And then I bowed my head, creating my own whirlpool, and my glasses leapt from my face and I touched them briefly with my fingertips and then they were gone.

Bukit Lawang had been described to me as a sort of backpack travellers' haven, and even though I usually tried to avoid the batik-wearing global party kids with their guide books and their Caucasian dreadlocks, I now longed for easy conversation, and even, a little, for hash-fueled Dylan and Marley sing-alongs. And perhaps a small dose of holiday nostalgia. It was a poorly-timed impulse, though, because it seems that on New Year's Eve the prices for rooms go up, the backpackers leave, and the village is flooded with busloads of teenagers from Medan and Chinese and Malay tourists. I didn't anticipate this, and I was desperate not to spend my last night of the year in Berastagi, a depressing and apocalyptic place surrounded by smoking sulfurous volcanoes, inhabited by the most embittered casualties of a tourist economy.

It was painful to remain a simple tourist in Berastagi, but it was impossible to be anything else. The town's main feature was the noisy crowded road that ran into town and ran out. In a sad street market where every stall contained exactly the same souvenir key-chains and wooden carvings, I was trying hard to maintain a friendly disposition. I greeted a woman with *selamat sore*, good afternoon, and she smeared an ingratiating smile across her face and condescendingly asked me something I didn't understand. When I hummed in apology for my modest linguistic efforts, she mocked me.

There must have been a military garrison nearby, because I often saw General Wiranto's men loitering on street corners, rifles slung over shoulders. They were always having a good time — laughing, wrestling one another, going to the movies in their mirror sunglasses. People liked them — likely because they protected civilians from the police — and a small mob of children always accompanied the good-looking soldiers. When I went into the *kantor pos* to mail a letter, there was an impromptu squadron of three teenage recruits harassing the woman behind the counter. They fell silent while I wordlessly bought my stamps. The woman, young but older than these khaki-clad boys, avoided eye contact and spoke in clipped, embarrassed syllables. The soldiers slouched against the wall under the framed photo of Suharto, holding their guns the way I've seen teenage punks hold a squeegee. I said *terima kasih* to the woman, turned to go, and then I too avoided eye contact as three pairs of sunglasses watched me leave.

I woke up cold from the altitude in Berastagi this morning. The smell of bananas frying in the common room, the very thought of breakfast, made my stomach whimper and I maintained a careful fast for fear of becoming nauseous. Nausea is a constant travel companion, like a kid always whining to go home to his own bed, pining for the familiar. When I had recovered sufficiently from lack of sleep I flagged down a bus that said Medan and perched on a sack of rice, hemmed in by kids and grandmothers and the stick-shift, so that I had to lift my feet in the air each time the driver changed gears. The two boys acting as footmen rode the roof rack along with my backpack or clung to the side of the bus, yelling and swinging, manic yet nonchalant. Then at Pinar Baris bus station in Medan I found a bus going to Bukit Lawang and took the last seat, but by the time we were trundling into the jungle the bus carried at least fifty more people, packed in the aisle and clambering on the roof. When the bus stopped at the entrance to the National Park, a man in a drab Park Ranger uniform and a mustache got on, said a few words in Bahasa Indonesia and came straight to me, the only white person on the bus. He said that everyone entering the park must buy a ticket, a claim undermined by the busload of people around him who were very obviously not buying tickets. I had been warned of this little charade — in truth, Bukit Lawang is not actually in the park — and I told him so. He persisted, and our little confrontation quickly became the center of attention, exacerbated by shouts and jeers from the other passengers which made him nervous and more aggressive. I didn't know who was being jeered, he or I. He suddenly turned with a scowl and moved along the aisle, making an extremely sloppy and transparent pantomime of selling tickets to other people, who co-operated half-heartedly by pretending to have money in their pockets. He finally shrugged and got off, waving his little ticket book over his head.

It was around 3:30 PM when I got to Bukit Lawang, sweaty and hungry. People on the path into the jungle saw my backpack and informed me that all the hotels were full, which at first I didn't believe (usually the touts try to convince you that theirs is the only place in town with vacant rooms) but which turned out to be true. First I asked a rosy-cheeked German couple on their way out — the price of their room had been suddenly inflated and they were heading to Medan. Then as I was passing a guesthouse near the bus stop where I had wanted to stay, a guy with long straight hair in a ponytail flagged me down with a friendly 'hi' and a chin-bobbing gesture. "You look tired," he said. He was wearing round silver glasses — very similar to mine, which are now being ground to a coarse shale by stones in the river. I asked him if he knew of any places with vacancies and he said no, but offered to let me share his room at the guesthouse. "I think I took the last room," he said. "Looks like we picked the wrong day to arrive." I had been handed an ad for a new tourist lodge on the edge of Bukit Lawang, located thirty minutes walk into the jungle. I hadn't intended to go there, but now it seemed I had little choice, since this new dentally-perfect friend was just a little too gregarious for me to handle in my fragile state. He wished me good luck and gave me a friendly slap on the shoulder.

I still had eaten nothing except a handful of peanuts I bought from a kid on the bus, and my energy was already depleted. It was so much hotter and more humid than Berastagi had been, and my clothes were drenched. My back was sore under the weight of my pack, which felt like it was actively trying to knock me down and get away. As I eased it to the ground my shoulders began shaking uncontrollably while my legs turned to rubber. Hordes of people passed by as I sat by the path, feeling dizzy. I wished that someone would pick me up, carry me to a soft bed with clean sheets under a cool breeze, shut the door and sit beside me. Watching me sleep.

I left my pack in the lobby of the last hotel in the village proper and set out for The Last Resort. The path became a skinny mud track alongside steep hills and across slippery bamboo bridges, through miniature waterfalls. Campsites were blossoming by the river. Every Indonesian guy who passed me said, "Hi Mister, Where are you going?" or sometimes just, "Where are you go?" One guy had not learned the entire phrase yet and just said, "Where are you?"

When I finally arrived here I was offered the room of an

employee who apparently does not intend to sleep tonight, at the top of a precarious flight of concrete and bamboo stairs, which require a daring and nimble leap between the concrete part and the bamboo part. The room is actually dark and attic-like, a six-foot by six-foot plywood box, but to me it looked truly transcendental. I said I'd take it, and then I sat for a moment.

The Last Resort is new and looks impermanent, perched on stilts as if afraid to touch the ground. It's built of deep red, knotty jungle wood in the Batak style, like a giant ship floating in the grass, hovering over what was once a bar of gravel in a bend of the river. The first floor restaurant has no walls, so that the rooms above with their blank plywood construction look like a huge treehouse nailed together by a pre-pubescent Frank Lloyd Wright. Down by the river a bunch of people were gathered — the owner told me that orangutans come down to the water on the other side, to watch us watching them. I thought about leaving my pack where it was until evening, but I knew that would be unwise, and I wanted to take a bath in the river immediately and put on fresh clothes. I knew that the walk back into town would exhaust me. I didn't know if I would make the return trip without collapsing, and I began to vehemently resent my backpack, as if it were some dislikeable person who had died and I was expected to carry his leaden remains to their distant final resting place.

My dread of the return trip is all I will remember of it; when I found myself back at The Last Resort, the inert carcass of my belongings draped over my shoulders, my short-circuited memory had already erased those thirty minutes. I dumped the backpack in the room. Took out a towel. Drops of sweat from my forehead, making it dark. My neck hurt. Soaked. Dizzy. I put off eating. Just to wash off, to cool off. And then to eat. I took off my boots, my clothes, my glasses. Remembering the orangutans I put my glasses back on. I couldn't find the soap. I found the soap. I jumped down the stairs in my bare feet and scraped my toe. Not good, bleeding feet in the jungle. I limped tenderly over the rocks. People along the bank, laughing. I didn't see any orangutans, didn't care. Couldn't think. I waded in. The water was cold and very fast. I crouched. I braced myself against the rocks. For a moment, I could see the future. As if I were standing on the bank, watching myself. I still had a few fingers on the edge of the cliff, but I was going to fall and there was nothing I could do. I thought, I am no longer in control of my body. The sunlight reflecting off the water confused me. I was both above the water watching, and under the water being watched. I was sad already. I submerged my head.

It was bright under the surface. The water rushing noisily, blocking out sound, pushing my glasses up my face and over my head. I grasped, lost my balance, the river tipped me over. Pushed me along a few feet, bruising my tailbone and then scraping my knees as I tried to stand up. My feet down. I stood up. The river was now a deceptive surface of shimmering silver, smooth black rocks and flecks of quartz on the riverbed, everything imprecise. Everything took on a sore, strobing intensity, merciless and relentless. I didn't swear or say anything. Instant amnesia.

8:00 PM. *In the jungle it's dark: hostile, and unknowable, except to those who have evolved here. It seems a paradox at first, that something so much like a living organism should be so persistently deadly. But it is self-explanatory: there is so much life here that the competition is poisonously fierce, and when wayward humans like me wander into the tiger-and-tarantula-infested jungle we realize how unfit we are, how fragile compared to everything else. I feel undoubtedly malicious micro-organisms battling me in obscure corners of my intestines. Here, an hour of muddy walking from the nearest telephone, another hour by bus from the nearest doctor, jungle stretching out around me for days, so thick and barbed, my mind begins to* *transform my surroundings into a gigantic, unsettling metaphor. But the forest is only itself. The micro-organisms are inside me; I carry them around with me. The jungle has penetrated inside me too, and that is what I was afraid of.*

Now the ants, invincible in their numbers and their confusion, have taken this page as well as the table I'm sitting at, and I feel considerably more fragile by comparison. I trace their trajectories with my pencil, but I can make no sense of the pattern. The plunge in the river has left me shivering and my skin feels strangely tight and uncomfortable, while my limbs are weak: like a baby, or else an extremely old and decrepit person. It's all my fingers can do to hold a pencil to paper. Thoughts of malaria or other feverish illnesses are lurking on the perimeter of my feeble consciousness — I imagine them crouched behind the thick trees around the clearing. But the onset of ordinary physical symptoms, and the blessed gibberish of delirium, would be almost a relief.

After my glasses disappeared, I stood squinting into the water for a few minutes. I took a few steps, stumbling and feeling with my hands among the rocks. They must have sunk, I said, maybe out loud. They must have sunk and they must be here, somewhere, I said, pulling up twigs from under stones until I realized the futility of the situation. Behind me, upstream, the laughing voices were becoming louder and I wondered for a moment if they were laughing at me. Then I heard swishing and snapping noises above the roar of the river, and I saw the jungle move: the huge trees across the river were swaying in and out of focus. Then one bent far out over the river, and the blurry people cried out and pointed up into the foliage. There was a reddish-orange blur in the tree, high up, swinging from a branch like a huge plush key-chain dangling from a rearview mirror. Another tree was shaking further up the bank. The orangutans had come to see us, but I couldn't see them except as phantasmagoric blurs. I needed to use my hands to climb up the muddy bank. My towel was a blue puddle in the grass reflecting the blue sky. I began to descend into a suffocating, thick, exotic depression like a feather-bed with no bottom.

I made it back to my room, crawling rather than leaping over the gap in the stairs, my toe starting to sting. I forced myself to get dressed, to come back down, and I managed to suppress the lump in my throat long enough to ask for some tempeh satay and some ginger tea, although now I no longer feel hungry or see the point in eating anything. Some tiny rational voice in my mind is trying to tell me that this sudden and severe gloominess, this lack of will, comes simply from exhaustion and hunger. But it is like trying to save a drowning person with verbal commands. I can hear it calling, I can even see its lips moving, and although I have a good idea what it is saying, the voice does me no good.

My tempeh has arrived and I have tried to eat it while the plate is hot to deter the ants. It's too heavy and greasy but I eat most of it before I become nauseous. Now the first ant is making a foray onto the dish, examining my peanut sauce. Finding it palatable, he goes to report to the others, or maybe the spices have him lightheaded, because now he is wandering aimlessly over the table. I'm sad, little ant, and you seem sad too. You don't know where you're going. You get to the edge of the table and you can sense the immensity of the abyss with your feelers. Maybe it's because this year is past, or maybe the thought of facing the future is exhausting. Maybe I fear being abandoned in the oblivion of the present.

This is the way I usually feel on my birthday. Birthdays have always been tearful interludes for me, since my 18th, that first year away at school, walking in the snow on the lawn of U. Hall. I remember being astonished, and worried, at the ferocity of my depression that night. Holly Joy was with me; it was only a few months after I had met her and Seth and Laurie at the newspaper.

At that point I had no idea how depressed she was: I didn't know that she had cut her wrists over Christmas, just a few weeks before, or I would not have expected her to say things to comfort me. She did, though: she asked what was wrong and I said nothing or I didn't know. I was leaving one era and starting another, of which H.J. was clearly going to be a part, and suddenly I felt it viscerally. The era I had just left, looking back, seems so cramped and bland and marred by fear and insecurity. H.J. saw this a lot more clearly than I did. She was listening to the Smiths and was acutely attuned to the malaise of teendom in the eighties, her parents being ex-hippie professionals with twin Toyotas. Meanwhile I was just discovering Simon and Garfunkel. I must have sounded ridiculous to her, but she didn't say so. We lay in the snow until we were shivering, then we went and found Seth and crawled into bed with him.

The result of writing this melancholic lament is that I am literally sick to my stomach. I have to seriously consider the possibility that I am ill, which wouldn't be so surprising, but the night's celebrations are already starting — I can make out bonfire sparks glowing through the trees along the river — and I hate the thought of needing medical help on New Year's Eve in the jungle. There is no light in the toilet, or in my room or on the stairs, the jungle is closed over our heads like a tarpaulin. For the next twelve hours I'll lie down, or fumble about in the dark getting sicker, and maybe my head will stop spinning. Now I'm feeling all shaky, and my knee hurts. All I'm trying to say is that I'm scared, fuck, and I don't know what to do.

January 1, 1997. 12:30 PM. The Jungle Guesthouse. *In a hammock you can be away from everything, not just the ground. In this particular hammock, on the second-floor balcony of The Jungle Guesthouse, Restaurant, and Tube-rental in Bukit Lawang, not only can I pick my feet up off the world and suspend judgement, I can watch the world moving away from me in an orderly line, as the local party-ers roll up their* *tents and head back to the city. The path to the bus station passes right under the balcony, and as the humans file past carrying packs many times bigger than they are, I can trace their progress, hidden behind a tall leafy banana tree. I can only see them as blurs, but they can't see me at all. I am filled with a suspiciously grand sense of relief that they are leaving, that the party is over, and that now this green year is already half a day old.*

The Jungle Guesthouse is an architecturally amazing place, more like an outgrowth of the jungle than a building, crammed haphazardly between the path and the steep hill rising from the river. The tables in the restaurant are all made of jungle wood, as are the walls, the window frames, the staircase to the balcony and the balcony itself. I came here first thing in the morning and ended up moving in with Cedar, the guy I met on the path yesterday. The room is across a bridge from the restaurant, with a small window looking out on a gurgling waterfall surrounded by orchids. There are tiny shelves carved into the bedposts and walls, and gauze curtains around my bed (my new roommate insisted on sleeping in a hammock slung across the room). It is all so paradisical that I am slightly unnerved, as if I have arrived on Fantasy Island and someone may chastise me if it is discovered how miserable I am. So I have taken my white rice and ginger tea and retreated to this hammock on the restaurant balcony. I am also in hiding from Cedar.

Cedar is the first Westerner I have had a conversation with for quite a while — he sat down with me this morning while I was eating a piece of bread and told me his name, wished me a happy new year. His breakfast was three bowls of steaming porridge, a plate of pineapple slices, and a cup of thick coffee with the grounds floating in it. The smell of the coffee alone was enough to make my bowels jumpy. Cedar is from Portland, it turns out, and has a broad smile that he keeps on standby at all times. The name is of his own devising, I learned. Cedars, he said, represent his place of birth. I asked him what his name used to be, but he said he'd rather not tell me, that it was a part of his process.

He has been travelling for almost two years, living off money that he won in a lawsuit from a CEO of a major logging company. He told me the story. It seems he was canvassing for Greenpeace and had the misfortune to knock on the door of this CEO, not knowing who he was. Not surprisingly they ended up getting into an argument, with the CEO pursuing Cedar down the street, and then somewhat more surprisingly the CEO pulled a gun and made threats on Cedar's life. Cedar had the presence of mind to step in front of an oncoming car, which stopped, and the CEO was scared back to his house, and the next day Cedar found a lawyer and took the man to court for assault. The story had a decent American ending; Cedar was awarded a towering stack of green and the local branch of Greenpeace was overjoyed with the publicity. Now he has recently arrived in Indonesia from Malaysia, and intends to volunteer a few weeks at the Orangutan Rehabilitation Center.

The mandate of the Bohorok Rehabilitation Center for Orangutans is, in a way, to help the apes adjust to the alienation of modern life. In Indonesia it has long been a tradition to give a baby orangutan to important people as a thank you gift — a gesture that now occurs less frequently but is all the more prestigious given the scarcity of baby orangs. Usually the only way to get a baby orangutan is to kill the mother, and this, along with the dwindling size of their rain forest habitat, gives orangutans a lot to feel depressed about. The Center finds orangutans that have been living in captivity and buys them (although often the owner is quite willing to part with the full-grown version), and attempts to reintroduce them into the wild, here in Bukit Lawang. The problem is that the orangs have no notion of how to start a new life or any fierce desire to do so. They keep hanging around the center, constantly coming back to the feeding stations for warm milk and bananas, checking up on their human friends and bumming cigarettes off the locals. They don't know what to do with themselves.

"Did you know that *orangutan* means 'man of the forest'?" Cedar asked me. I told him I did. I had been planning to go to the Center today myself, I said, but yesterday I lost my glasses in the river and now I can't see anything. I didn't say that I also thought that visiting the Center would be too depressing.

"You lost your glasses too? That's *so* funny — you know, I knew when I sat *down* that you and I had something in common," said Cedar. He had lost his glasses in the river a few days ago. He had been on an inner tube at the time, as people here often are, and got capsized in some particularly vicious rapids. He says there are dangerous undercurrents around some of the rocks, and he figures he almost got killed. I had to admit that I had not been tubing. He told me that he went to a nearby town called Kuala, where there is an optometrist, and he got his new glasses the next day. The bus goes there every afternoon around two, apparently.

Cedar wanted to know how I had spent New Year's Eve, and why he hadn't seen me around. "I had an amazing time last night [he admitted]. The owner here — he's very cool, a really amazing, *really* nice guy — invited me to go to this *tent* some of his friends had set up on the river bank, over where the bat caves are, where there was a *party* going on. There were a couple of guitars and some drums, and we just played music all night, and smoked this a*maz*ing grass that somebody had, which, you know, usually I don't do much, but these guys, they were so super, really friendly, and I just felt really safe, you know? It's funny how you may not be able to speak the same language but you feel entirely comfortable anyhow — you know what I mean? It was a really amazing feeling, and this morning as the sun was coming up we walked over to the caves to watch the bats returning. It's an incredible sight. I was in awe. The bats were returning to sleep, while everything else was waking up to a new year. It was like the jungle had just been born."

I told him I was sick last night. "That's too bad," he said. "Listen. I hope you don't mind me saying this — my friends say I tend to perceive these things a little too quickly — but you look like you've got a lot on your mind, and you might need someone to talk to, and I just wanted to let you know that I'm willing to listen, if you want to talk. Come and find me any time." He smiled.

I said thanks, and that I had to go make a phone call.

I've just come back from New York, which is still suspended in that risky liminal moment of the first few hours after birth. The phone call cost me 50,000 rupiahs — about the equivalent of my entire food and lodging budget for the past week. I talked to Seth, and Pascale, and William, asked them to repeat themselves repeatedly, listened to them singing along with a million or so other humans in the street. I sat in a booth behind a glass door, watching the little stopwatch turn that would tell me how much to pay. I was expecting to reach them in the apartment, soberly eating pretzels and playing Scrabble, but William answered amid crowd noise. "Well here we are live in Times Square," he said in a Dick Clark voice when I asked what was going on, "and let me tell you the excitement of the crowd has reached a fever pitch. Seth, I don't think I've ever *seen* a New Year's Eve crowd of such astounding proportions. In just a few minutes I think we'll be ready for the countdown, and you can feel the anticipation — Seth?"

(Pause, phone changing hands. Distant cellular voice.) "Hello, is that you? Are you okay? How are you?"

I told Seth that I was okay, for the most part, and then told him about my incredible stupidity in losing my glasses while trying to bathe. Then, obviously forgetting that I was on the other side of the world, he asked me if there was some kind of celebration going on. I looked through the door of my booth at the little room of the Wartel office and the bus sitting on the road outside. The young man at the desk was eating a plate of nasi goreng and watching a small black and white television. There was a woman with a microphone on the screen, surrounded by seven-foot tall transvestites on roller blades, with a big Times Square clock in the background. I reminded Seth of the temporal anomaly in which we were sharing, accentuated by the lag in the phone line which made it seem like we were in different dimensions, imperfectly aligned. He asked me how I had spent New Year's Eve and I said mostly vomiting and shitting. He related this news to the others.

Pascale immediately interrogated me on what I had been eating, wanted a complete description of my symptoms, accused me of not drinking enough re-hydration mixture and suggested chewing on papaya seeds. "We've been worried about you — Seth and I." She then wanted to know what my plans were, where I was going next, and I told her I hadn't a clue. By then it was time for the ball to drop, and William interrupted her and held the phone in the air between them while they all sang "Auld Lang Syne", and I watched the scene on the little TV in the Wartel office. William came on and said Happy New Year and sent me kisses, there was confusion and kissing noise for a while, and then Seth returned.

"I'm a little confused, Seth."

"You sound it. Can you see anything without your glasses?"

"No. I'm going to get new ones this afternoon."

"Are you feeling better this morning?"

I told him that I no longer felt like I was going to die, but couldn't really say that this was an improvement. I don't know what to do now, and I realize that years could go by like this, wandering. I half-hoped, I said, that I would meet someone or start something here. I had been looking forward, for some reason, to starting the new year in Asia.

"The continent of the next century," he said. He suggested that perhaps I had plunged my head into the river on purpose. "You know," he said, "I've noticed that it's at times like these that things like that happen."

The call had lasted twelve minutes already and that was all the money I had in my pocket so I said good-bye and Pascale wished me a happy birthday, "In case we don't talk to you before then." I walked back against the tide of the departing crowd. I had intended to tell them something about the last day of the year, and how the world looks strange and fuzzy in this new light. But twelve hours is a large cultural gap and how could they understand?

When I finally closed my book last night I felt something inside me move. I struggled up the broken stairs to my bed, stripped off the scratchy *ikat* blanket and lay down on the bare mattress. Immediately my guts began to clench, so I stood up, holding the door-frame to keep from falling over the balcony, and made it down the stairs again like a two-year-old, sitting on each step and lowering myself to the next one with my arms. The *mandi* was on the far side of the building from my staircase, so I opted to go between the wooden piles underneath, rather than limp through the restaurant clutching my stomach. This *mandi* was an unusual Siamese twin: the large square reservoir of water was shared by two tiny rooms, each with its own concrete hole in the ground. A wall of translucent fiberglass divides the rooms, but over the reservoir it only comes down to within an inch or so of the water's surface. The familiar plastic dipper sat on the ledge of the reservoir. In the dark, the placement of the door handle, the touch of the fiberglass at my back, and the sound of invisibly splashing water: all was transformed slowly from frustrating trial to mechanical routine, finally transcending that to become reassuring ritual, as the diarrhea became worse and worse and I felt myself become weaker and more dehydrated. I don't know how many trips I made, but each time I followed the muddy path under the building, moving from column to column for support, the way the orangutans move from tree to tree.

The noise in the restaurant above grew steadily. The bonfire by the river was getting higher, and it seemed more people were arriving at the party upstairs. Coming out of the *mandi* I saw the man whom I had paid for the room, carrying an armload of bottles. I knew him by his whistling, since I could barely make out his form, but when I first met him I had noticed that he was probably younger than me, dark with curly hair and a brilliant, teenage smile, alluringly handsome. His name was Jelli. I stopped him and asked him if he had any bottled water and he said he did and I asked if he would get me one and put a pinch of salt and a few spoons of sugar in it and he said he would and then he asked if I was sick and I said yes I'm sick and he said you look very bad and I said yes and he said he would bring the water to my room. He came up soon after and knocked gently and gave me the water and said he had put a little lemon in it too so it would taste better and I said thank you and he said if there was anything else I needed I should ask him, and when I felt better I should come to the party. Then he pointed out to me that there was a small kerosene lamp on the wall and matches on the shelf, and he left.

Almost immediately I had to get up again, stumble down the stairs, under the floor, to the fiberglass room. A sarong is an efficient item of clothing when necessity demands constant squatting, but even with it hitched up around my waist it soon got wet as I blindly doused myself with water from the *mandi,* so I took it off after a couple of trips and left it in the room. There was a light breeze from somewhere brushing my naked legs, and the air and the water in the *mandi* both seemed to be exactly the temperature of my body, and I began to feel completely undifferentiated from the night as my insides also turned to liquid. The trips down the stairs began to blur into one another like Duchamps' *Nude Descending a Staircase*. At around ten o'clock, on my way through the forest under the building, I was very quickly overtaken by an extreme wave of nausea and immediate, violent regurgitation, ending in a coughing/choking fit as hot, sour mucus dripped from my throat. Afterwards I felt somewhat better.

In the *mandi* I saw through wet, bleary eyes that someone had put a candle in the other compartment, so that my side was filled with soft green light that flickered through the fiberglass. It was a little like being under water, for which I was glad. The puking had made me light-headed and I started to feel like I was having a dream. There was someone in the other room, making almost no sound, and I could make out an outline of a shadow crouched just on the other side of the wall. It was the first time all evening that another soul had shared this familiar space with me, but in spite of my pathetic state I found it not embarrassing or uncomfortable but reassuring, to find someone that close, with nothing separating us but the fiberglass as I leaned against the wall. There was a lengthy, intimate silence. Even if I only whispered, the shadow would hear everything. I could hear soft breathing. There was no way to know whether it was a man or a woman. Then the claws in my intestines struck once more, and I sighed involuntarily, feeling helpless and insubstantial. This time, mercifully, the pain emptied from my body, and I shuddered, exhausted, but finally somewhat purged. A hand was dipping into the water, throwing long slender shadows into my cell, quiet and graceful. I dipped my own hand into the *mandi* and washed myself ritualistically. Silently, deliberately, the figure behind the wall stood up and I heard the rush of the fabric as a sarong fell about someone's knees.

I lay down on the mattress in my room and could not move from that position, could not light the lamp or hang my mosquito net even though I could feel tiny filament legs brushing my forehead. Meanwhile a segment of the party had moved into a room two doors away, singing and speaking exuberantly, so that I could hear every word they said, without understanding any of it except the occasional joyful "Hello! How are you!" Songs floated up from below also: someone with a guitar was playing "Yesterday" over and over again, slurring all the words completely except for that one. I drifted off to sleep and back again many times. People passed in front of my door, and at one point I'm sure someone even knocked, and waited, and knocked again. In my dreams, I answered and told him to come in but there was no reply.

In semi-consciousness, I came to the realization that all other noise had stopped and that everyone was singing "Happy Birthday" in English, in unison. Failing to reach any rudimentary understanding of why this was happening, I became worried that I had forgotten something important, that I needed to be somewhere. Then I remembered: it was H.J.'s birthday, but she had forgotten to invite me. When I got out of bed and tried to find my glasses, a bunch of men came into the room and insisted that I needed to buy a ticket if I wanted to cross the river. Two of them, who were actually no more than boys, clambered into bed with me and when I tried to put on my glasses they put my hands between their smooth brown thighs and held them there. They were accompanied by an orangutan who carried with him a device that would make me Indonesian, after which I would be able to breathe under water. The apparatus was complicated and rather elusive, but it involved a kind of mask that would prevent me from seeing or make me see around corners. It had a bulbous bumpy handle like an avocado, which the boys kept trying to put between my legs. We were on an inner tube together, floating down a river but not the Bohorok river. There were cities on either side with hundreds of billboards, written in languages I couldn't identify but whose meaning I understood clearly enough; they all wanted me to go to some hotel, where I could choose from a range of machines that would make me any nationality I wanted, and there would be rooms filled with crisp, cool snow covering everything, that I could lie down in and pull over myself like a blanket.

Throughout the night I woke up periodically, came part of the way to my senses, and wanted to know what time it was or what year it was. I looked at my watch, but since it was pitch black in my room I couldn't really see the face. I mistakenly thought it was around three when they sang "Happy Birthday", and I peered at my watch later and it seemed to say seven. I went back to sleep and woke up again at nine, and then ten-thirty, and then I dreamed that there were ants all over the bed, and I sat bolt upright. A thin light was sifting into the room. My watch said 6:30, and already I was coated with a thick, moist heat.

(Same day) 1:30 PM. *Just came back to my room at The Jungle Guesthouse. In half an hour I'm getting the bus to Kuala. Cedar is a very trusting person, or else very stupid. In fact, I think he did this in order to demonstrate that he trusts me and that I can therefore trust him. I don't feel like analysing the complex motivations that may lie behind this gesture. He left me in the restaurant and went off to the Center for the day, and when I came back to the room there was a wad of money lying on the table, as well as his camera bag and what looked like the contents of his waist-pouch, including his passport. I ignored this little display at first, but then I had a sudden compelling rush of curiosity. So, checking first to make sure he wasn't coming, I picked up his passport and looked inside. I don't know how to feel about what I saw. His real name, the name that he felt compelled to shed at some traumatic point in his life, is also my own.*

(Same day) 6:30 PM. Bohorok Dokter Mata (eye doctor), Kuala. *Sitting outside the office now, on the side of the main street on the outskirts of Kuala, waiting for the bus, and it's starting to get dark.*

The sky is still pink off towards the jungle. I must have drifted off in the heat, and I was dreaming that John was still here, and Cedar too, and Jelli from The Last Resort, but my stomach is clenching again so I woke.

I was just about to climb the ladder to the roof of the bus when John tapped me on the shoulder. "Excuse me, mister, let me do something for you. We will pat each another's backs." He was smaller than me, but not so small for an Indonesian man. His hair fell down to his eyebrows on one side, his face was slender with dark eyes, and his clothes were ordinary but striking somehow — blue button-up shirt and white pants — perhaps because they were polyester. I wondered where he got that phrase, which had never been used on me yet. I asked him what he had in mind. "You will ride in my car where you want to go, and in return you will listen to me speak English and that is all. If you want."

It sounded suspicious enough that I said no at first, *terima kasih*, but when he immediately apologized and left me alone I knew he was probably on the level, and so I got off the ladder and followed him. He was glad to see me. "It is better for you to the car, I think. Do you know the roads are made in dirt? Maybe you like to eat dirt? For lunch, maybe. In your teeth." He squinted and grinned as if wind was blowing in his face. He was very cheery.

The car was actually his brother's, who was driving but who didn't speak any English and didn't say a word throughout the hour-long drive. John and I sat in the back. I told him my name and asked his, and he told me and then introduced his brother, whose name was Matthew. He explained that they were named after the books of the Gospel, because his parents are Christian, and he had one other brother named Luke and a sister named Mark.

"I know, this is not usual, a sister's name is Mark. But my parents can not speak English so they named her just because they are Christian. I call my sister Marcie. I am Christian, of course.

Are you Christian? Many Americans love Christ, I know." I told him that I wasn't American and thankfully he didn't seem too interested in pursuing the question of my religious affiliations. John's family, he went on to say, was Batak, the ethnic group that lives around Lake Toba. "Many Batak are Christian, but in Binjai or Medan there are not so many Christians and mostly Muslims. But I like Islam. I like the *hijab* those womans have on their heads. I think it is pretty. They always make a good style, I think."

John is a student at a university in Binjai, but I couldn't really make sense of his major. Something about business, but involving international politics. "But I don't like it," he said, dismissing the subject. "Actually my hobby is theatre." When I told him I had studied theatre myself he grew even more animated and started telling me about the project he was working on. "Actually we are making an opera, and our theme is about the student. So we played an examination's situation, and a student who cheated and caught up by the teacher. Ha! I always smile to remember this. Can you imagine it? I am the director."

It turned out he wasn't kidding about the you-will-listen-and-that-is-all promise. He was intensely enthusiastic about his own life, and it was jarring to my ego to meet an Indonesian who didn't want or need a thing from me. When he grew tired of trying to explain the opera to me, he decided to give me lessons in Batak. "That way, I can explain in my language and you will understand finally," he said. He wrote it all in my book.

English=Batak
Horas!=Hello!
Thank you, Thanks. =Mauliate.
Thanks a lot, Thank you very much. =Mauliate godang.
Do you, Did you, Will you speak English?
=Diantusi ho do bahasa Inggeris?

(Batak is like Bahasa Indonesia, John explained to me, and has only one verb tense for past, present, and future.)

I love you. = Holong rohakku tu ho.
Do you like/want (to) me? = Olo do ho tu ahu?

As he read the last sentence, he gave me a nudge and said I could use this sentence with all the pretty Batak girls I would meet if I went to Lake Toba, and they would be very impressed. He had a sly grin on his face and kept repeating the phrase for me. "This is very important, Mr. Corey! You must to learn this! Just imagine! Maybe you have a girlfriend already? Many girlfriends, maybe." I smiled and shook my head. He was silent for a few minutes. We were passing through a rubber plantation and I looked out the window at the rows upon rows of slender trees, all carrying little cups around their waists which would fill with thick white sap.

The car was Indonesian-made, one of the ubiquitous compact sedans that is practically the official car of the country. The manufacturer is owned by Suharto's nephew, like most companies here that aren't U.S. multinationals. The ride was no less nerve-wracking than the roof of the bus would have been, as Matthew followed the Indonesian customs of passing trucks around corners and driving on whichever side had the fewest potholes. Occasionally he would yell at a passing bicycle something I assumed was an insult or an expletive, but John completely ignored him and kept on talking about verb tenses or costume design.

When I told him that I was getting out in Kuala, and explained that I wanted to see the optometrist to get new glasses, he warned me that probably the doctor would not speak English. Cedar had told me he did, but John insisted on coming into the office anyway, and we found out that in fact the English-speaking eye doctor had gone away for New Year's. It was that doctor's father who talked to

John, a *dokter mata* himself who hadn't learned the business from English books, and he was willing to see about some glasses for me. He was an ancient-looking, wrinkled man, little more than half as tall as I am, hunched over, with a small white fez on his head and glasses thick enough, it seemed, to stop cosmic rays. Even if I could speak Bahasa Indonesia, I wouldn't have been able to understand him because he spoke as if his teeth were rattling about in his mouth. John offered to stay and act as a translator for me, and immediately ran out to confer with his brother, who I saw give a simple shake of the head which means yes. The car pulled slowly up the street. "He will find to eat," said John.

The *dokter mata* addressed John with a clipped sentence and he answered in a few words, to which the old man nodded sagely. Then he beckoned me into the back room, where there was a formidable apparatus. The lights were dim enough that I could not really see into the corners of the room, at least not with my present ocular abilities. In the center was a throne bristling with optical devices, various pedals and small lights and a few chrome toggle switches. Its simple design was from before the era of plastics; keeping pace with improving technology was probably no more important to this *dokter mata* than it is to an executioner, and in fact the apparatus did have more than a passing resemblance to an electric chair. It had narrow leather slings for arms, a padded head-rest, and individual metal foot-rests for each foot. Its main feature, though, was the massive chromium boom, on which were mounted two wide black disks with eye-holes on the inner side of each orbit and a metallic beak that I guessed would rest in front of my nose, all of which gave the machine

the appearance of a gigantic cross-eyed mechanical owl. The *dokter* invited me with a gesture of his hand to step into the seat. Once I was seated, he had to stand on the foot-rest to reach the owl-face's handle, which had the shape and dimensions of a hand grenade. The unit was even bulkier than I had first thought, and as he pulled the eyepieces in front of my face, the handle descended to waist-level and I felt pinned. The *dokter* turned out one light, leaving us in the dark for a moment, and turned on another which illuminated a scrolling paper screen. He then perched himself on a high stool next to me.

The entire examination proceeded along these lines: the *dokter* would utter a laconic command or question, which John then translated so that I could respond *ya* or *tidak*, and John filled in all the spaces with an on-going monologue which the *dokter* would occasionally acknowledge by a wag of his head or a grunt. The only word I occasionally understood was *mata*, which means eye. After the *dokter* had clicked through a series of lenses for each eye and after I had identified the tops and bottoms of numerous three-legged table icons, he pushed the owl-mask aside, stood up, and walked back into the front room without a word. John had obviously been paying attention, because without consulting the *dokter* he immediately explained to me what I had always known: "To see the small things is okay, but you have a problem to see very far."

In the front room, the *dokter mata* indicated with a sweep of his arm a glass-topped counter which contained all the frames available. There were no Yves St-Laurent three-hundred-dollar models, and I couldn't see any John Lennon-style wire rims either. I'd had it in the back of my mind that I would try to find frames like the ones I'd lost: something that would allow me to feel like I was me again. But these were all strictly utilitarian: thick silver squares with spring-loaded arms, transparent plastic rims that looked like safety goggles, or plain black ovals with wide McCarthy-era temple-guards. I had almost settled on one of these vaguely retro-hip fifties styles, even though I was certain they would make my nose look artificial, when I noticed another display case on the other side of the room. I glanced at the *dokter* and gestured at it, moving over to take a look. To my surprise, he wagged his finger and stuttered disapprovingly. "This case is only the styles for the women, he says," John told me. The tiny man had already scuttled around the counter and was putting his arms over the glass as if to prevent me from seeing what was displayed there. But it was too late; in those few moments while his guard was down John had already stepped over next to me and had seen the variety of curves and colours in that other case. "Mr. Corey!" he practically bellowed. "These glasses make a much better style, do you think?"

The women's frames were more adventurous in general: there were corners pointed like French curves, tiny glass jewels set in the rims, glittery gold arms, and thick plastic in translucent beige, fuchsia, turquoise, maroon. John exchanged a few rapid words with the old man, who initially put up a what seemed like an impatient argument, but then reluctantly opened the case and took out whatever caught John's eye. Most of the frames were hideous, but there were others that were simple, more refined than the men's frames. John picked up a pair of tortoise-shell frames that had "Diana" written in golden script on the inside of the arm. "I think this will make you very handsome," he said as he lowered the arms onto my ears. I would never have considered buying them on my own, but even as I thought this I realized that they were exactly what I wanted and needed. Something that was not at all what I had come to believe was me.

6:45 PM. "*It was musical opera. The opera played with music. The lyrics were not connected with the dialogue, but the musics. At that musics we played ballet. We can only understand the show after the show's finished.*"

(John's explanation of the show he directed at his university.) I still don't entirely understand what he was talking about, but it sounded postmodern and adolescent and campy all at the same time. "Well, I don't know how to explain it if you don't understand, yet!" he told me. "Just imagine!"

Across the street is a small brick building behind a fence with a tidy lawn, and I can't read the sign but it appears to be a *kantor pos*, a post office. Next to it is a two-story house, which maybe belongs to the *dokter mata*. At the top of a high post next to the gate is a shape that I'm guessing is a cage, because within the shape, I can tell by its singing, is a *burung*, a bird. Further down, that long low building with the paved yard is probably a *sekolah*, a school. The town is a filmic blue. There is movement near the center, and groups of men standing around what appear to be *truk-truk*, trucks, but this stretch of street is mostly deserted. A couple of boys in dirty white t-shirts were on the opposite corner for a while watching me write, but they grew bored and went away. One of them left what I think is a *sepeda*, a bicycle, behind that gate, red and yellow and blue. Since I got to Sumatra I have been sick with the monotony of seeing the same familiar, unfamiliar things again and again. One advantage of myopia is that all those things must now be re-identified. At the moment, a small white peripatetic blur is lurking in a nearby alley. My theory is that it's a chicken.

John and Matthew have left, and I'm waiting for a bus to bring me back to Bukit Lawang. The *dokter mata* said I should come back tomorrow to pick up my new glasses. He handed me a card and John asked if I would get lost. I told him I would be okay, and I asked him to write his address on the back of the card, and then I tore a piece of paper from my book and although he didn't ask for it I wrote down my address in Montreal and gave it to him. We shook hands, and John said may God bless you and I said break a leg, and he laughed and said, "Break a leg! Yes, I know that words!

I always think it is funny. I wish we would break our legs."

Matthew was waiting in the car with the engine running, and John got into the back seat, then he rolled down the window and leaned out. "Happy Birthday," he said.

"My birthday isn't until the 22nd," I said.

"Yes. I know. But did you know? In Korea, everybody's birthday is on this day. Today every Korean is one more year old. I read it in one encyclopedia."

"Yes. I went to Korea in the Spring."

"You travel to so many places. Why do you want to do it?"

It had thought it was obvious. But I can't even remember much of what I did in Korea, at this point. I have already forgotten large parts of 1996. "I don't know," I said. "Because I think it will help me understand things better."

"Well, good-bye," he said, and the car pulled away. He waved. "I hope you will understand things, Mr. Corey!" They drove off towards Medan in a cloud of dust and I sat down on the curb.

Now the ants who live on this dusty concrete sidewalk, worlds away from the ants in the jungle, are coming to visit me, carrying bits of paper under my legs and around the corner. Maybe they are putting the pieces together and constructing a book off in the bushes behind the garage. They don't seem so interested in taking over my page, these ones. The page is trackless and white like a field of snow and wants to be filled. Eventually, a blur comes along that I take for a bus, and I get on it whether it is or not.

January 2, 1997. 7 PM. *Got back yesterday at nine. Cedar was waiting for me. He asked me how I was, and I told him. This morning, we both went down to the Rehabilitation Center and signed up. I met my first orangutan close up; he was in a cage, sticking his fingers through the bars, touching them to his clownish lips. I realized he wanted me to give him a cigarette. The first step, I said to him, is admitting that you have a problem.*

Tom & Jerry, on the ferry

I'm on the ferry between Dover and Calais, which the sign says is the busiest ferry crossing in the world, although I very much doubt that is true anymore, now that trains are snaking their way through the tunnel under us, the tunnel with the slightly embarassing name. The mouse from Tom & Jerry (Is it Tom? Or Jerry? I can never remember which is which.) has just snuck up behind me and tapped me on the shoulder. I turn around slowly, and somehow I manage to be unsurprised that a giant mouse is smiling and waving at me. I wave back at him. In my mind I have maintained some dignity, but the people around me laugh at me anyway. I am suddenly worried that he will try to start a conversation with me, and I don't know if the official language of the ferry is English or French. Instinctively I wonder, "What language does a six-foot tall anthropomorphic mouse speak?" I have not spoken French seriously for two years, and I have perhaps some anxiety about the difficult linguistic situations this trip might place me in, communicating with life-size cartoons being one of them.

Of course, he doesn't speak any language — he's just some poor teenager with a shitty job in a hot fuzzy suit, who must remain mute for the sake of accuracy to character, and perhaps also out of embarassment. The mouse mercifully disappears and I return to writing in my book, but about ten minutes later the cat shows up. (Jerry? Tom?) He's cavorting with a little boy on the other side of the cabin. Perhaps Tom and Jerry are really the same person, under their fur. Perhaps that explains why they are never seen in the same place at the same time. The French coast looks as though it would fit into the coast of England perfectly, like a jigsaw puzzle piece, or else we have simply sailed out of sight of the white cliffs, and then turned around and sailed back again. For most of today, I will not be anywhere in particular.

Coming

I am sailing back over the channel to Dover, singing songs in my head. I have been to Paris, I have gotten drunk on the steps of the *Oratoire* in Montmartre, I have risked death crossing the traffic circle at the Arc de Triomphe, I have lost my shoes on the Champ-de-Mars and gone home barefoot on the Metro, I have seen the dismembered third finger and thumb of *la Victoire de Samothrace* on display in a glass box in the Louvre, and I have met a beautiful young Parisian woman on a train who tried to seduce me, and I still don't know why she was unsuccessful. Against my own better judgement, I have paid incomprehensible amounts of French money for the privilege of having toast served to me on a sidewalk by goofy-looking young men who act as though they have more sex in one month than I have had in my life, which is probably true.

An announcement has just been made that Tom and Jerry will be appearing shortly on the dance floor in the bar, "*pour danser avec les enfants.*" They will only be there for a few minutes. It is a revelation to me that the cat and mouse are not simply opposed aspects of the same essence, a plush yin/yang, matter/anti-matter, but rather discrete corporeal entities that can exist simultaneously in adjacent space. I don't stick around to witness it with my own eyes, though; instead I slip into a small room near the stairs with round windows looking out on the English Channel. One row over is a tidy young man with an angular face who occasionally looks up from his guide book at me. Eventually he comes over and asks me if I am going to London, and if I could give him advice. His name is Roberto and he is from Italy. His plan for the summer is to find a job in a London pub, even though his English is abysmal and we quickly switch to French. When I tell him that I stayed in the Marais, the gay quarter of Paris, his eyes sparkle with interest. He stayed there himself, just the night before, in a disco bar, he says. He asks me where I am staying in London.

I am enjoying this conversation, the idea that I may be flirting with Roberto even though I am sure I must be doing it all wrong, the idea that one can suddenly, while crossing a body of water, be presented with the possibility of becoming a corporeal entity distinct from the one you've always known. All the way to England we exchange stories, and Tom and Jerry dance by and wave at us and we wave back and then grin at each other, but once we have landed on English soil, in the immigration lines, we become separated; he disappears into the faster but longer line for Europeans, and when I come out the other side I wait for him for a good long while, but there is a train to catch and besides, sooner or later, I mean, really.

Mencontek

A musical opera. (The opera played with music.)

The opera is played with a male and a female. We took some of the female to be male. There are total nine in the dialogues but these maybe different people and signing musics. The musics and all the dialogues had already recorded and just acting on stage. The music originally played and sung by the real singer, but we recorded from their album. We took some short musics and lyrics from different musics. We made the dialogue in the middle of the musics before the next musics. Between the dialogue and the musics are not really connected each other (some yes). But what we played depends to the dialogue and the musics. At that opera we took some Indonesian's song "Mencontek" for example. And we took some English musics. The musics can be any chose. We can only understand the show after the show's finished.

The theme is about students. The act starts with some students at their first time in the University and ended with examination. We took Indonesian's song "Mencontek" which means "cheating". That is the beginning.

["Mencontek"] >> "cheating". This is everybody, Ballet.

In the room there is some table and chairs. Only there is a map on the wall (world's map). There is the teacher, then there are the students. It can be many students, but 3 is alright.

Student number #1 "Johnny" [our hero]: Is this the class for the Geography?

Teacher [it looks like woman]: Yes.

"Johnny": Geography is boring! I don't want to be very boring!

Teacher: Are you "Johnny"? [Yes]

Teacher: It is because you are famous now, with your dance move and everyone thinks that you are very very sexy. (Another students are come in the room) **Teacher**: Then, everyone sit down. [sit down]

Student number #3: Yes, ma'am.

Student number #4 "Suharto": I don't want to sit down to there. I want to sit in this teacher's chair.

Teacher: You must to sit down.

"Suharto": My father owns this school and he owns you and your father's office where your father works.

Teacher: There is some foreigners here now, so that doesn't matter so much. This country is an University, this is not high school/junior high school.

"Johnny": You are a student the same as us, so sit down. I don't care what your father owns. Your father is Soekarno and he owns the whole country because he invented the country so he owns it. You did not invent anything, so you can't tell us what to do. Sit down.

"Suharto": I am angry at you, Johnny!

"Johnny": After this class we will have a contest. I have a car outside.

"Suharto": Me too!

"Johnny": You should be careful, Suharto! [they sit]

Student number #2 [a very beautiful female student]: (she thinks that Johnny is sexy).

Teacher: Thank you, Johnny. You are very brave and after this class I want to see you (she wants to tell him that she is in love for him)...

Gulliver's Travels

It's just like travelling to any place on earth, really. Some days are easy, and some days are worse than you could imagine. I had brought with me a rather superfluous device, a small tape player with a tinny speaker. When it played tapes they dragged, and the music sounded as though it were being squeezed from a tube like toothpaste or fake cheese. It also had a radio, but I certainly didn't need it, because walking through town you could hear radios blaring from every open window. There was only one station, so as you turned a corner and the song faded from one window, you could pick it up from another window farther up the street. For the sake of concision let's call this radio-cassette player simply "the device".

Almost every day I had been going to the travel agency. It wasn't until a week later that I realized that the husky-voiced woman behind the desk was actually a man. She had a penchant for flowery sun dresses and a different colour nail polish on each finger. I had been assuming that she was just flat-chested. Let's call her "Rosemary". She got to know me, and to a lesser extent I got to know her. "My country owes your country a lot of money," she would say to me. "We will pay you back soon, I promise. Do you want a cigarette?" No, I would say. I just want that four billion dollars.

In the safari park there was a polar bear, of all things, stretched out like a rug on a concrete beach. He looked yellow, like he'd been smoked. He was probably from Canada too, I realized, and he didn't like the heat any more than I did. I watched him for ten minutes or so and he didn't move, but occasionally he would lick his chops, as though he was suffering from a great thirst. After a while I noticed a movement in his pen, off by the bushes that hid the fence. It was one of those feral dogs with the pendulous teats. I don't know what she was doing there. The dog trotted over to the polar bear and started eating his food. The bear lifted his head for a moment, but then dropped it to the concrete again. Let's call the polar bear "Richard".

On the way back from the park we drove through a shantytown where some kids were diving from a low wooden bridge into the muddy water. One of them, I noticed, was missing a leg, but he could still dive. We passed a store that sold only bananas, and another store that seemed to have only eggs. Then, as we rounded a corner, we came upon a silver tank truck with a single word in large black letters on the side. I don't speak the language, so I have no idea what the tank actually contained, but what it said was "SEMEN". I thought to myself, this has all the makings of a well-managed population explosion. We'll call the one-legged boy "Arthur."

Later that day I came into Rosemary's office with the device hanging from my belt. My tickets had not arrived. When she saw the device, her eyes grew wide and she motioned for me to sit in the plastic chair in front of her. From under her desk she produced a shoebox filled with bootleg cassettes of local pop stars, and she asked me to play one. When I realized that she had nothing to

The global economy is operating noiselessly.

play them on, I spontaneously decided to give her the device. She seemed to need it more than I did. We'll call that "my first mistake". Then I had a salad for lunch. We'll call that "stupid".

There is no reason to be afraid of salad, in itself. Invariably, though, salad is either not washed, or even worse, it *is* washed, in water. Water, if it is not boiled or in a bottle, is definitely something to be afraid of. I like to cite that famous sign in the tourist restaurant: "All the water in this establishment has been passed by the manager." Salad is one of those insidious comforts, like ice cubes or air conditioning, which you assume at first to be on your side, because it reminds you of home or cools you off, but which then betrays you by giving you a head cold, or an anonymous but acute form of gastro-intestinal distress, as in this case. We'll call it "iceberg sickness".

I was riding on a little padded seat on the rear rack of a bicycle, passing through the poor part of town on my way to the Presidential palace. Under the steam of a small man in a white suit — we'll call him "Roger", the bicycle was wobbling creakily between small dirty houses and piles of garbage, dodging rampant pigs and children. I think that at first when Roger beckoned to me and patted the back seat, he had just been kidding. I was on his bicycle when the iceberg sickness kicked in, and I had to tell him to stop immediately — which he didn't understand until I put down my feet and dragged them in the dust, losing a sandal in the process. I gave him money and then I lurched off in the direction of a banana grove, clutching my stomach.

There was no time to go home, no time to search out a toilet, even if there had been such a thing in the town. My stomach was having a seizure. Nevertheless, modesty dictated that I wend my way through the forest behind a nearby house. It was a hot day and I felt rescued by the shade of the banana trees, their leaves as wide as my chest. When a boy is in love, I thought to myself, it's just like being in the middle of a banana jungle. Everywhere you look, there are big bananas, everywhere. I laughed at myself a little, but then felt another agonizing pang and had to immediately drop my pants. I was standing in the middle of a neglected garbage pile, featuring rusty cans of Fresca and plastic bottles that said "air".

As I squatted, the contents of my intestinal tract making a daring daylight escape from my body, along with valuable ions, I realized that from my new perspective closer to the ground I could see through the trees to the road below, at the bottom of a small incline. It was a wide but empty back road, running alongside an empty field. Already the heat and dehydration were making me dizzy. The flies were relentless in their thirst for the sweat on my arms and face, but the chickens pecking around in the garbage seemed prepared to ignore me. Each time I thought I could stand, I was soon stricken by another bout of cramps. I had been there perhaps twenty minutes when I saw someone in a bright yellow dress coming down the road, dancing. It was Rosemary.

As she got closer I saw, and then heard, that she was carrying the device in her hand, singing along to whatever it was playing — I couldn't really tell because at that distance the music was just a high-pitched buzz, as though she were dancing down the street with an electric razor. She had a purse on a strap over her shoulder. Out from behind her desk, she looked a lot taller, but her feet were not as graceful as her slender hands were when she would pass me a brochure with a flourish. But then, she obviously did not think anyone was watching. She was approaching the bend in the road opposite my secluded bunker. In the meantime I was being accosted by a pig, which we'll call, oh I don't know, "Wilbur".

Wilbur had appeared among the banana trees without warning and was rooting on the far side of the rubbish pile. He was a large, barrel-chested animal, not chubby and pink as one imagines the ideal pig but black, gaunt, and disturbingly bony, with bristly hair all over his back and shoulders and a desperate, stupid look in his eyes. He immediately started behaving in a way that made me think he was dangerously deranged: after staring at me for several minutes as if trying to hypnotize me, he took a few deliberate steps towards me. I reached for a rock and he grunted and retreated among the leaves.

When I looked at the road again, Rosemary was surrounded by a pack of perhaps six or seven young boys, of varying heights and ages. I don't know where they came from, but it was obvious that they were not her adoring fans. At first they were just walking next to her, taunting her maybe, although I couldn't hear (or understand) what they were saying — maybe they were singing. But then — it happened very quickly — two of the boys were trying to wrestle the device out of Rosemary's hand, and she was resisting, yelling at the top of her scratchy voice, kicking and slapping at them.

The most amazing part of this story is that right then a police car came along. There was something bizarre and corny about the timely appearance of the police, as though we were in a badly scripted movie. The kids saw the car before I did and scrambled in formation across the field, with Rosemary hurling insults after them. One boy did not run off but hobbled along the street on a home-made crutch — it was Arthur, the one-legged diver. The car stopped and little policemen began to get out, seven of them in total, tumbling out like clowns from a jalopy. Some of them wore uniforms, but others were only identifiable as police because they matched the others in size. Rosemary was taller than any of them.

Wilbur was advancing towards me again; I couldn't figure out why but it made me angry and nervous. "Screw off, bacon-face," I said. The iceberg sickness was not as acute, but I was still losing liquid, and feeling helpless. Down below, the smallish officers of the law had surrounded Rosemary. They were laughing with one another, and one of them had taken the device away and was playing with it. Rosemary looked panicked and was not saying a word. One of the men kept lifting up her dress. The one who had the device suddenly turned up the volume all the way, and then I could hear what was on the cassette; it was that Bryan Adams song that was so popular on the radio just then. "Everything I do, I do it for you," it said.

A grunt from Wilbur reminded me that he was getting awfully close. He was a huge, tough-looking beast, and I wasn't feeling all that self-confident. What if it came to a physical struggle? What did this pig want from me, anyway? I picked up another rock and threw it at him, this time striking him in the hindquarters as he lumbered off squealing. Now Rosemary was being pushed toward the car. She was trying to get away, that was clear, but they had her arms firmly twisted behind her back. One man shoved her against the far side of the car; all I could see was her head above the roof of the car, and the men standing in a circle. Rosemary was disconcertingly quiet. Then she disappeared behind the car.

I felt like I might faint. I wanted to do something to help her, but just as I was about to pull up my pants my bowels burst open again. My throat was as dry as cement, and I wanted to vomit but I couldn't. With my head in my hands, I heard the slamming of car doors. The song ended abruptly. I looked up to see the car driving away, with the seven diminutive policemen inside and Rosemary too, and I thought, how did they all fit into that tiny car? It was astounding. The street was now empty, except for Arthur who was sitting at the base of the slope, facing away from me, his crutch lying on the ground next to him.

When another fifteen minutes had passed, the iceberg sickness had run the worst part of its course. I was far from well, but thought I could make it home. I left behind me, where I had squatted, a nauseating puddle as evidence of my corporeal instability, a mephitic icon of my mortality. As I pulled myself together, having made use of a discarded dishtowel, Wilbur stared at me. He's fascinated, I thought. He has found something more pitiful than he is. I half-heartedly threw a rock and missed, then took a couple of steps up the path. Wilbur shuffled behind me, and then I heard a lapping noise. The pig was hungrily licking up the fetid mess. In a moment, another pig arrived on the scene, even bigger than Wilbur, grunting and jostling for position. We can call this second pig "Alice" if you want.

I had only gone a few steps when I heard a car stop on the road below. Crouching, I looked through the trees and saw the police car driving off in the direction from which it had come. Rosemary had been ejected and was standing on the shoulder, trying to straighten her dress, her hair. Her purse and its contents were scattered on the road around her. The device was no longer in her possession. Momentarily, she threw a fit of sorts, swinging her fists and shouting at the car, which was gone. Eventually, though, she sunk to her hands and knees and started collecting her things. I hesitated, wondering if I should go and help her.

The week before I had gone to the ballet in a gymnasium, where I sat in a folding chair in the second row, the turbaned head of the man in front of me blocking my view. I couldn't see the dancer in the middle, but on either side of the turban floated two identical dancers. My conscience was now acting in the same way. I should go down there, said the figure on my left shoulder. It would just humiliate her, said the one on the right. I thought, also, of the doors to the old palace, guarded by two identical warrior statues, one of which represents good, according to the tour guide, and the other evil. I asked which was which. Well, he said, this one is maybe good. Or maybe this one. They are identical, so nobody knows.

I noticed another person on the road below. Arthur had gotten up from where he had been sitting and was teetering slowly towards Rosemary, showing incredible co-ordination in his one-leg/

one-stick method of locomotion. About ten paces from Rosemary he stopped and watched her until she noticed him there and looked up at him. He was holding something in his right hand, leaning on the crutch with the other. For a long moment they regarded each other, as if they were on intimate terms. Finally Rosemary said something to the boy, which may have been anything but which seemed to me neither friendly nor vicious. Arthur didn't respond, except to draw back his right arm and throw a rock at her, hitting her on the shoulder. He turned and left.

That's the story; let's call it "Gulliver's Travels". I don't suggest that because of the Lilliputian police or the Brobdingnagian pigs, nor do I mean to imply any political allegory, nor make any smug allusion to Swift's notorious scatological obsessions. Everything has to be called something, even if at times it feels like the act of naming is a vulgar, facetious satire. I went to the police to register a complaint: harassment, robbery, battery, rape. I checked all the boxes, which was strangely satisfying, even if I suspected it was utterly futile. I didn't go back to the travel agency, though. Call it what you like, but I couldn't bring myself to see Rosemary again. I had planned to stay in town longer, but I knew it was time for me to leave when I returned to the safari park and visited the polar bear enclosure. Richard was no longer there. There was no explanation, just a sign that said, "Coming soon: Penguins!"

A small complicated underground city

The night of the storm I am alone in my apartment. The plastic I bought at Canadian Tire is just beginning to peel off the windows and I have decided that I'm not going home for Christmas. When the power goes out, I say, I'm thinking of a person; you tell me who the person is. It's like those games you've played where people take turns asking, Are you an animal? Are you a movie star? Are you alive? and you answer, Yes I am, No I am not, Yes I am.

C'est une question un peu bizarre, peut-être, mais... c'est que... je voudrais savoir... la voix qu'on entend sur la système, la messagerie vocale... c'est qui?

Pardon? C'est qui?

Oui, c'est qui, cette voix?

I am a real person. I am alive. I'm not famous. I woke up at 2 PM one day and had an experience which upset my routine, so subtly and yet so powerfully that it caused me to re-evaluate the series of occurences that I had until then regarded as my life. Although the beginning was sudden, the experience took a year to happen completely, and by the end I was wondering, How did I get here? Where do I go from here? and also What will I leave behind when I go? By the end, I — that is, the person I'm thinking of — was also thinking of a person, because a mystery is often solved by another mystery.

Oui, c'est qui, cette voix?

Mais, je ne sais pas vraiment. C'est... je suppose que c'est une actrice. Cette une voix enregistrée, vous savez. Ou bien quelqu'un qui travail ici.

I have a telephone. The experience I'm thinking of began while checking messages on this telephone — it's a service provided by the phone company which obviates the necessity for an answering machine, which itself obviated answering the phone. The telephone is located in an apartment with a metal staircase outside, high ceilings, hardwood floors, and two balconies, and in the winter there is never enough heat. On the day I'm thinking of it was particularly cold in the apartment, and when the phone rang repeatedly I stayed in bed. The bed is a well-worn futon with mismatched quilts. A ringing telephone is a difficult stimulus to resist for some people, but I'm indifferent to it and it's the city I'm thinking of that fosters that indifference. When I did get up, I found there was no more coffee.

Oui, je suppose, mais je voulais plutot savoir le nom de cette personne, ou si je pourrais parler avec elle.

Mais, elle n'est pas ici! Je sais meme pas son nom, et si je le savais je ne pourrais pas vous le donner, pas de question!

Pourquoi?

Perhaps many people had called that morning, or maybe it was the same person calling over and over, but there was only one message, and all it said was "Where *are* you?" What caused my *bouleversement* was not the message, or at least not the content of the message. It was the frame that caught my attention: the voice that says how many messages there are, usually as familiar and unnoticed as my own, had been changed. Before, it had been professional almost to the point of condescension, and slightly robotic. But this new voice was real and nuanced. It said exactly the same words, the rhythm and even the intonation were unchanged, but the difference was unmistakable.

Pourquoi? Parce-que si je vous le donne, il faudrait le donner à tout le monde, à toute la ville.

C'est une question un peu bizarre, peut-être, mais... c'est qui? (Basically, the speaker wants to know the identity of the person on the voice-mail system. French is not the speaker's first language.)

We seldom actually listen to the words on the system. It's only the first time that we actually hear them. "To listen to your messages, press 1" conveys an instruction essential to the operation of the system, but once we know the routine, there's no point in having these words repeated. The system therefore allows them to be truncated like so: "Listen, press 1". The phrases become abstract sounds that elicit certain specific responses. In this way, "Listen, press 1" is removed from the context of the linguistic system we associate it with, and becomes instead a functional element of a different system, the voice-mail system. Responses are in the form of precise machine sounds: if you want to send a message, you press "2" and the device makes a sound that corresponds to "2". If the system allowed, the words themselves could be replaced by iconic beeps, and the ear would interpret them just as easily.

Pardon? C'est qui? (Casual bewilderment. The *téléphoniste* has a stressful job. She's probably been told to give a false name if anyone asks for it — in fact she has one all picked out. Giselle. She can't tell what is being asked, and maybe she hasn't decided whether or not this is harassment.)

I had stopped listening to the words. I did not interpret the words as human communication anymore. No one does. So when I found a different voice speaking them, it was as if I could see directly through the words to the personality. The words became transparent, not because their meaning was readily apparent but in the opposite sense: the words had no meaning, they were simply the substance of that mysterious identity, located not even at the other end of the line, but somewhere between this end and the other end. And what made this new voice, this new identity, different was that it acknowledged the meaninglessness of "Listen, press 1." The voice was saying to me, "You and I understand one another. We both know what's going on, and it has nothing to do with messages."

> *Oui, c'est qui, cette voix?* (Here, a touch of paranoid defensiveness. The person speaking is likely unsure whether the confusion is due to the question itself or the imperfect French in which it was rendered.)

> *Mais, je ne sais pas vraiment.* (She doesn't know who it is. Really. Pause.) *C'est... je suppose...* (An actress, or somebody who works here.)

But something else caught my attention. This new voice was a familiar voice, so familiar that at first I hadn't even noticed how easily it fell into place in my mind. Could it be I knew this new voice-mail voice, knew her as a whole, embodied person?

> *C'est juste que je pense que c'est quelqu'un que je connais... et j'aimerais savoir comment la rejoindre...*

Perhaps I had just heard the voice many times before — the same person probably does the voice-mail system at work, or maybe it's the same voice that says "Watch your step" at the airport. I was reminded of an incident, when I met someone on the street whose face I knew very well, yet whom I couldn't identify. I smiled at this man and said *bonjour*, and he nodded back, but it wasn't until later that night when I went to the corner depanneur for cigarettes that I realized he was the man behind the counter.

Oui, je suppose, mais... (Can I talk with her, the caller wants to know?)

Mais, elle n'est pas ici! (The *téléphoniste* hints, through metalinguistic cues, that the person calling is a lunatic.)

A few days later, when it was too cold to go out, I spent most of the afternoon phoning all the electronic systems I knew — the university, the library, the train station — but none of them answered me in that voice, and I couldn't remember where I'd heard it. Gradually I became convinced that it was someone I knew, or had once known. Over the next few weeks, as the city thawed and I went about my meagre "business" again, my conviction wavered like a mirage, but it finally solidified right in front of me and blocked my path.

Pourquoi? (Why?)

Pourquoi? (Why?)

C'est juste que je pense... (It may be an old friend. The speaker would like to say more, but is beginning to feel the futility of the task.)

I tried to imagine how I might contact her. The question seemed absurd, since every time I picked up the phone, there she was. Every time I wanted to contact someone else or someone else contacted me, she was the messenger. But I couldn't send her a message. She had no name, no number. I could not dial V for Voice.

Mais c'est impossible.

The first few times I called the phone company I was completely rebuffed, but finally I convinced someone to take my name and number and to pass a message on to her. By this time, I wasn't sure if I really did know her, or if it was just the voice I knew. I wondered if I was one of those frustrated individuals who fall in love with celebrities and then try to get their attention by killing other celebrities. My connection to the voice could, I suppose, be described as an obsession. But it was nothing as deluded or foolish as "love". It was simply that this voice, with its confident pronouncements and its reassuring cadences, made me feel better about my life as a non-celebrity.

Je ne peux pas vous promettre qu'elle va vous appeller.

Je sais. Je vous remercie.

About a month later, I got a message. I'd been home all day, and the phone hadn't rung. It had been dark for hours when I realized that all I'd had to eat that day was a bagel with cream cheese, so I picked up the phone to order some food; I was surprised to find it was beeping. A message had been sent directly to my voicemail, as if it emanated not from a distant telephone but from somewhere within the system itself. It was definitely the same voice, but the effect of hearing it speak spontaneous words was surreal, and it also seemed like two different people because of the two languages. She left no name, no number. And no indication that she recognized me from her own past.

> *Bonjour. C'était une des téléphonistes qui m'a donné ce numero. She told me that you believe you used to know me. But well, I must tell you, c'est une période très difficile pour moi. I have tried to... sever... all contact... avec mon ancienne vie. J'éspère que ça ne te fait pas trop de misère. I hope you will not be offended. If things go well, maybe I will phone you. But I can't promise. Please, je ne veux pas que tu essaye de me trouver. Goodbye.*

And that was the last thing I heard her say to me. Which is false of course in at least two ways, because I continued to hear her voice every day on the answering service, and because even this message was not her, it was only another recording. It was, in

The snow appears to fall more slowly than usual.

a way, more "real" than the recording I always hear, and maybe it's the only thing I ever really heard her say. But sometimes I feel like this "real" voice is coming from another world entirely, and the only voice that is really her, for me, is the one telling me, "You have no new messages." One voice was natural and the other supernatural, but I couldn't tell which was which.

I played it over and over, paying attention to how the nuances of the voice corresponded to those on the system. It had a distinct vocal signature — certain vowels pronounced certain ways, certain words liased — just like a written signature, or the marks made by a particular typewriter. But the voice also diverged sometimes from its little rituals, and in those hesitations or sudden changes of direction between languages, there was a momentary escape from the persona performed on the system. In those moments, when the language blew open like a curtain in a window, I thought I saw a glimpse of the person I used to know. I couldn't see the face, only a familiar shape — intimately familiar, even: not just an acquaintance, but someone I had, in some way or another, loved. It was a boy, a very peculiar boy I had met one summer, not here, but I wasn't sure where exactly. I vividly remembered his skinny frame and the soft short hair at the back of his neck, but when I tried to picture his face the curtain blew closed again. Neither could I put a name to the shape, or any linguistic tags at all except a murmured phrase, an exclamation that was half laughter. No words would adhere to this person I'd been fond of, but the voice was unmistakable and clung tenaciously to memory. The pitch was different; it was now a woman's voice, and older, but it was not too different and I could hear in it that boyish laugh. Anatomically, there is not much difference between the voices of boys and women.

They were the same person, the woman and the fragmented boy. The different genders did not seem to be a contradiction. The voice was gendered, certainly, but like the words, the gender seemed arbitrary, a part of the user-friendly interface. The fact that the voice was female, I realized, was not accidental: voice-mail systems are always inhabited by women. It's as if they live there, in a grey room surrounded by fibre-optic cables, situated somehow within the network of phones and wires, the walls lined with voice-mailboxes stacked like pigeonholes. They sit in cubicles, dressed in skirts and blazers, and at lunch they eat dainty sandwiches at their desks. At night they sleep curled up in the boxes. They constantly make recordings of themselves, and it is the recordings that live in the real world. When we get our messages, the voice on the phone becomes one of those women: sitting behind her typewriter with a nail file, receptive, non-threatening. Answering phones is, after all, a secretarial function. But when I try to picture her, I always see Dustin Hoffman in *Tootsie*. Or Miss Piggy. Wasn't it Frank Oz who played her voice? Like a conspiracy theorist, I felt I had stumbled on to something I wasn't supposed to know. Maybe the voice on the phone had been digitally altered. Or maybe the boy I had once loved was only a boy in my memory. The more uncertain I became, the more I wanted to meet this person — not because I wanted the mystery to be resolved, but because it excited me.

But she didn't call again. The summer came, rather unexpected for me as it is every year. My mind and memory played with her identity and found a place for it, but did not put it away. Everyday I listened to her voice religiously, and when I picked up the phone I felt an instant sense of well-being. No matter how many times I listened, beyond the functionality of "Listen, press 1" the voice was always saying something different and intriguing to me.

I don't know when exactly it started, but sometimes, when alone, I would indulge in a kind of dream-like sexual meditation while listening to her instructions. For some reason it was easy to imagine a real person talking to me on the other end of the line; but because it was someone I knew, I found it much more thrilling than any 900 number. I would turn on the speaker-phone and wander through the menus. I especially liked to press 4 — for personal options — and record a greeting as if I were speaking directly to her, and then she would play it back to me. If I waited too long before choosing an option, as would inevitably happen, she would gently remind me of her presence and ask, Are you still there? And if I still neglected to press anything, she would tell me she was sorry I was having problems and ask me to try again later. I'd had phone sex before, with real people I had known, but this I thought was a whole new kind of telephonic intimacy. It was not like having sex with someone else through the medium of the system, it was like having sex with the system itself. I felt, for a moment at least, that this was somehow historically significant. But then I thought, what if other people in the city were doing the same thing — perhaps even at the same time? I slowly had to admit that this was entirely possible. Even assuming that a third of the city's population doesn't subscribe to the system or just doesn't have a phone, two million people still hear her voice every day: more than the audiences of the radio personalities, the Musique-Plus VJs, the late-night psychics or the phone sex operators. Her voice is easily the most famous person in the city, and yet no one knows her name. Surely there are people in the city who simply have no other voices to listen to. Or nothing else to do, or no money to do it with. At first, I thought the pang I felt was jealousy, but eventually the voice's anonymous fame only made it more seductive.

When you send a message to someone, after dialing the person's number you hear the person's name or else you hear the voice-mail voice saying, "*Système de Montréal* — Montreal System." Now I feel like that system has been linked directly to my nervous system, my ears and mouth and the respiratory system that causes my own voice to work. It has fused with the rest of my life and the rest of the city. One unusual day in the Fall I was riding on the Metro — unusual because I had actually left the island, had exited for a few hours the scope of the Montreal System — and absently studying the lines on the map, blue and orange and green and yellow criss-crossing like a car's ignition wires. I re-entered the perimeter, sneaking up on the city from underneath as the train slid under the *fleuve*, the water a part of the Great Lakes-St.Lawrence Seaway system and the sewage system at the same time. The train, also a part of the system, continued into the section of the city's body where the digestive organs would be located. Then, flowing with the crowd through the doors and down the hall, up the escalator to another artery, and surging through a tunnel lined with cables for the electric system, the phone system, the cable system, the water system: the enormity of the infrastructure struck me. (It's this infrastructure that has failed in the storm, while the plastic peels off my windows. If an element of the system ceases to function, the entire system is affected. As in language: without the rest of the system, the individual element can have no meaning. I'm going to light some candles now.) Without the system of desire I have built around myself — that is, around the person I'm thinking of — the words would have no meaning.

Montreal is a language; the whole city exists as a system of differences. This is most self-evident on the telephone, where every interaction begins with a choice: 1 for French, 2 for English. The arbitrary correspondance between word and meaning is demonstrated and celebrated on everyone's outgoing message, where every thought is deliberately spoken twice in different ways. With some of my friends, it is the only time I ever hear them use their second tongue. The Montreal System is a meaning mill: it processes bits and pieces of language and at the other end it churns out a city. (Just before the power went out, I called my friend, but she wasn't there. Her outgoing message said, Leave a sample of your voice in the receptacle provided, and we'll get back to you with the results as soon as possible.)

The end of the experience, near the end of the year, also came through the system. I woke up that day out of coffee again. I went out to find some and spent the morning taking pictures of the sunset on the mountain, since I'd missed the daylight entirely the day before and I wanted to preserve some of the fading purple sky in case I ran out later on. The sidewalk along Avenue du Parc hadn't been cleared, so I waded through knee-deep drifts in my sneakers, my wool socks adorned with tiny jingle bells of snow. I hid a paper bag of warm bagels inside my jacket and walked home in the dark. I had one new message.

Hello. You don't know me, but I'm calling on behalf of Kathy Tremblay. It's very important that you call me.

It was repeated in French and there was a phone number. I didn't know this man's voice, and I didn't know who Kathy Tremblay was, but I called back right away. The same man's voice answered, a voice that seemed perfectly real and responded to my questions. He asked me if I was a friend of Kathy's, and I said that

I hadn't seen her in a long time. He said my number had been in Kathy's address book, and he was trying to contact all her friends because, well, Kathy had died. The cancer had finally won, he said. He asked me if by any chance I was a relation, and I said no. So far he had been unable to locate any of Kathy's family. "I don't think that she was really in contact with her family," I said.

"Yes, so it seems. Well, the funeral is happening on Sunday." I took down the details and thanked him, and then as he was about to say good-bye I asked if he had known Kathy well himself. He explained that he'd been hired as an executor; he had never met Kathy, except once, over the phone.

After hanging up, and even during the conversation, I felt detached. Kathy was a name I didn't know and didn't even particularly like. Death is a physical effect and in this case an effect on a body which for me had never existed. In fact, the body had now finally attained a real presence; it was lying on a table in a mortuary somewhere, and soon it would be in a casket surrounded by flowers. Then it would be buried in the cemetary on the mountain. I could physically locate it and visit if I wanted to, on Sunday afternoons. But the voice was not with the body and never had been. When I lifted the telephone receiver again the same familiar voice greeted me and assured me there were no new messages. The recordings had not ceased to exist, of course; they are not re-recorded on a daily basis. For almost a year the voice had been saying these words to me, to us. Does the telephone company even realize that the original voice, the true voice, is dead? Her friends might find it disturbing to hear her every day on their phones. On the other hand, if a machine can simulate her existence long after she's gone, isn't that a kind of immortality? Perhaps fame is always in alliance with death somehow or other. It steals you away from yourself and fixes you in eternal, inaccesible space. Maybe this person is not the person who died a few days ago of cancer. Maybe, from the moment her voice was recorded, she was already dead.

I deliberated anxiously about going to the funeral. There would be nothing there for me, I realized; it would be like reading a letter over a stranger's shoulder. Still, I wondered who would be there. Curiosity and desire are as impossible to distinguish as extinguish.

The funeral home was only a few blocks from my apartment, a massive presence occupying a corner I passed almost daily. I had been aware of its function, but only obliquely, and the thought of entering the building made me see the corner in a different way. Stepping onto the sidewalk and staring the building in the face, I felt like something had changed in my relationship to the whole city. The exterior walls were stucco and seemed incongruous among the snowbanks. Tinted glass light fixtures glowed in the carpeted lobby, and waxy plants and a few raffia-wrapped chairs made it look like a Greek restaurant. It was the first time I'd ever been to a funeral in this city. I had no family here myself, and although people I'd known had died I had never wanted to take part in the organized mourning. I didn't associate the city with death, even though living here was a constant process of mourning something or other: someone leaving town, some job falling through, some restaurant closing. But now, in this space that was so intimate with actual death and reminded me of family, I felt like a completely new arrival again, a complete foreigner.

Opposite the front entrance, on an easel next to a pair of doors, was a black letterboard whose white push-in letters said "Tremblay". Next to it was a large sculpture of a telephone made of white carnations. Inside, about thirty people were sitting on metal chairs facing a lectern and a daïs where the coffin floated amidst a cloud of flowers. Across one of the larger bouquets was a banner which read, "Your voice will go on." Another one said simply, "Goodbye." The coffin was open, but I couldn't see her face; I could only see the lily in her hands. The service had already begun, so I sat down in the back row. A white-haired man in a clerical collar was standing next to the lectern, speaking about how tragic it is when a young life is cut short so abruptly. The mystery of death, he said, was evidence of God's glory, and he reassured us that if we looked to God, we would find meaning. The audience was mostly women, it seemed, dressed in sombre greys and and cream-coloured silk blouses. They were clumped together near the front, and I had the impression they all knew one another. Some of them looked to be in a state of shock. When the white-haired man stopped speaking, one of the few men in the audience stood up and went to the lectern. He arranged his suit jacket and then waited with his head bowed for what seemed like a long time before speaking.

"Je me souviens du moment précis quand j'ai rencontré Kathy la première fois... It was two years ago, when she came to work as a member of our team," he said. "I remember she was being introduced to me by a colleague from public relations, and this colleague was doing all the talking. But finally he stopped, and then I turned to Kathy and we shook hands and she said, 'It's a pleasure to meet you.' And I knew, from the moment that wonderful voice fell on my ears, that I would be glad I'd met her." He paused momentously. "Most of us knew Kathy as a colleague," he continued, "but we also knew her as a friend." Then, as if remembering something he had planned to say, he interjected, "Maybe not all of you knew what a good singer she was, though — as we learned at our karaoke night, last year at Christmas time." A few people laughed affectionately at this. "But every one of us, and indeed everyone in the city, although they may not have known her by name, knew Kathy as the voice who took their messages, a role that she filled with unforgettable flair. Perhaps we can be a tiny bit consoled knowing that every time we pick up a message, we will be reminded of Kathy. She was the kind of person who always had

a cheery hello or goodbye to get us through our day. She was an inspiration to us all, and I hope — no, I know — that she will continue to inspire even though she is gone, even though she has, in a manner of speaking, disconnected. Kathy has finally pressed *."

I could hear weeping from the first row. The man in the suit went on: "Before she died, Kathy wanted to record one final message, and she asked that the recording be played for everyone who gathered in her memory. So at this point I ask you to listen to Kathy's final words, following which I'd like to have a few moments of silence, to remember and cherish, and to inwardly respond to her words in our own individual ways." Then he nodded to someone standing near the back, and there was the low airy sound of speakers being turned on, and a moment of anticipation before her voice suddenly filled the room. I closed my eyes when I heard it, and with the static from the speakers I could almost imagine that she was speaking to me on the phone, speaking to us from the other world. She said thank-you to all her friends for their support through her illness, and expressed the wish that they comfort one another when she was gone. She said that in her whole career this was the most difficult recording she'd ever had to make. Her voice began to choke, as if tiny pieces were missing from it. She said I love you all, and then she said goodbye. The final goodbye was an echo of the one I had heard so many times after pressing * myself.

After a couple of prayers, a hymn, and a few more testimonials, the service ended and the other people started to file past the coffin, while I lingered at the back. I spoke to a few of the women as they drifted out the door. They were almost all secretaries, public relations people, and a small clique of operators. They all gushed about what a good friend Kathy had been, and how tragic her death was, but none of them had known her for longer than a few years, and they seemed to know very little about her past.

They knew that she was from a small town, but could not seem to agree on which one; that she had lived alone on the Plateau; that she loved to go out dancing on the weekends; and that she went on vacation in the Caribbean once a year. It was obvious that my desire to connect this woman to my past could not be satisfied by talking to anyone here.

After the room had mostly emptied, I finally gravitated to the front. She was wearing a blue velvet blazer over a high-collared, emphatically feminine dress the colour of a tropical lagoon. Her hair was auburn with streaks of blond, and curled in wisps around her ears. She seemed to be in her thirties. She had the complexion of someone who occasionally went to tanning salons, although it was difficult to see her complexion through the make-up. I didn't recognize her face. But there was no face in my memory to compare it to, so I wasn't convinced that this person was not the boy I had once loved. A familiar amalgam of curiosity and desire made me want to look beneath the lid of the coffin, and under the aquamarine dress. Are you a real person? Are you a movie star? Are you alive? From the face, with its cosmetic surface and its lips sewn shut, I couldn't tell anything about the rest of the body or the body's history. The system of gender had collapsed along with the circulatory and nervous systems — all the systems. But I was not obsessed enough to break all social and legal taboos; I had not gone that far. So I sat for a moment in a chair, and then I signed the guestbook. I felt compelled, for some reason, to leave a false name. Then I went home.

C'est juste que je pense que c'est quelqu'un que je connais... et j'aimerais savoir comment la rejoindre...

Mais, elle n'est pas ici!

For two weeks her voice continued to reassure me every day, and I made my own recording of it to be sure I'd be able to hear it whenever I wanted. Then it was replaced. I don't know how many times I called during those two weeks. I would sit and wait for her to ask me, Are you still there? And then I'd press a button and wait again for her to ask one more time. Are you still there?

Let's try this again. The night of the storm I am alone in my apartment. I am thinking of a person. Who am I? I am not the "I" of the previous story, but I'm not "me" either. I am not famous, but I am alive. My science fair project is a home-made computer. I made a grid of wires, and connected tiny red light-emitting diodes at all the intersections and connected the ends to little switches so that turning the switch for 2 and the switch for 3 would light up the light for 5, but it doesn't work, because I don't know anything about electronics or computers except how to write a program in Basic that will print my name over and over again until I stop it. When they came to my table I told all the judges that the batteries had died, and I still won second place because I had good posters. My computer has a shoebox keyboard, and if you turn it over it just looks like a jumble of wires, but all you have to do is connect this one to this one here, and connect this to the nine-volt battery, and all the LED's glow. Then you can imagine it looks like a small, complicated, underground city.

Horas! Mr. Corey

Thanks for the card, "Beautiful Paris" you've send. I like it. I am now mostly at home. We got a car accident, so we have to stay at home. But, actually we went to the Leuser. (Mount Leuser National Park) We stayed for two weeks there. It is very good, nice place. I like it.

What I can say about the weather now is "Ready". Ready to get wet, and ready to get hot. It is no more raining season. It is not yet dry season. Sometimes the rains come, but not so heavy. In June it will be hotter, +32 degrees.

But it is normal if the rains come by sudden.

Well, live in a healthy life.

John.

Blood and gasoline

From the Chugoku Expressway, we find the exit to Kobe. We enter the Shin-Kobe tunnel, on the way to the city, and it angles sharply downwards and the rows of lights disappear into the distance. It's an exact simulacrum of the experience of driving to the center of the earth. If nothing goes wrong, in the tunnel or in the story, we will resurface on the other side in nine minutes.

Furthermore, the story contains no accidents. Will anyone get hurt in the story? How long is the tunnel? Don't worry, says the driver. It's long enough, he says. But will anyone get hurt? I'm looking for a way that I can integrate myself into society. I like movies, but they aren't real. We will have to discuss the history of car accidents. For although there are no accidents in the story itself, they are a part of both the personal history of the author and the collective history which will influence our reading of the story. An anecdote about the author which will hopefully prove elucidating: It was a sunny winter morning with the world fading in and out like images on old celluloid. The author was only about three or four — in fact, this is one of his earliest memories. He lived in the country then, at the intersection of two busy roads. He and his older brother went out to play in the snow, and wandered down to the ditch. They were not supposed to play there, but on this particular morning in the ditch there were deep ruts in the snow, and various footprints surrounding a gouged-out area in the snowbank. The author's older brother said that there had been a car accident, but the author did not believe him. So he pushed the author face-first into the snow. It smelled like gasoline. Right in front of his face, in the footprints and in drips all the way up the side of the ditch, were red and rusty orange stains. It's blood.

A car collision is perfect. An expository car crash at the beginning is excellent foreshadowing, while the story begins with an idyllic situation. But the characters have one big problem. The problem causes all relationships to disintegrate slowly into a maelstrom of petty jealousies and simmering resentments. Then, near the end, when the problem is about to be resolved, a sudden car crash leaves one person dead and the others reeling emotionally. The shock of the accident causes each individual to undergo a profound questioning of self, and to gradually realize just how miserable they have all become.

The author has been in four two-vehicle collisions, three as driver. None of these crashes, however, were the author's fault. In car crashes, as in writing, nothing is ever the author's fault.

Although the story may concern real car accidents, this is no proof of its sincerity or its legal worth. A car crash always manifests itself as several contradictory yet simultaneous sequences of events, at least two and often more, depending on how many vehicles were involved and how many witnesses there may have been. It is impossible to specify a single chain of events as the definitive temporal reality for a given crash. The participants at this point must find a way to deal with the double trauma of material loss and ontological confusion. So they create in their minds a new crash, an ideal crash, which can be represented by a diagram on a legal-size sheet of paper, and in which blame can be apportioned by percentages. It exists only in the realm of the ideal form. It is perfect. The various people involved — the drivers and passengers, the police, the victims and their loved ones, the insurance adjusters, the lawyers, the mechanics, and the mechanics' loved ones — at some point will reach an unconscious consensus on the nature of this ideal crash, and they will then begin to worship that crash like members of an esoteric Gnostic brotherhood.

What happens if we want to turn around? Is the nature of the ideal tragedy so arbitrary that we can write it before it happens?

One

In the first collision, on Christmas Eve, the driver's head received a direct and abrupt introduction to the dashboard and consequently he was left with no memory of the events leading up to the collision or of the collision itself. Afterwards, as he lay in the hospital, the consensual details of the ideal crash were related to him: two cars, tangled in a snow-filled ditch like pretzels of steel, strewn with sixteen-year-old boys and smashed beer bottles. The only thing the driver could remember was that he was in love, and that he had a wrapped Christmas present in his coat pocket. It had become somewhat crushed. He could not, however, remember what the present was or whom it was for. This meant that the collision was even more perfect, since there were no pre-existing versions of reality in the driver's mind to contradict the description of the ideal crash.

How do we know that the same has not happened to us?

Two

A British writer has suggested that car crashes are intrinsically sexy, and those who are intimately familiar with automotive cataclysm can usually see the attraction; they understand the Dionysian rush that comes from speed, momentum, chaos. The second crash, however, was overwhelmingly characterized by not the erotic, but the comic. The driver had been in Osaka the day before, where he had seen a movie based on a book by the British writer mentioned above. He was threading along the mountain roads in a Honda Today, a car small enough for the driver to hug. In the opposite lane, moving at an imperceptible speed, was a tiny farm truck carrying two tiny people. There was a line of cars behind it, and it was slowing down to turn across the road. There was plenty of time for the truck to turn before the driver's car passed, but the truck did not turn. It slowed down and came almost to a stop. The driver got closer and cautiously slowed down, but the truck was obviously waiting for him to pass. The driver continued at normal speed. Then, the truck turned. It crept across the road in an agonizingly slow arc and the driver locked his brakes and glided across the asphalt, watching helplessly. Just before impact, he had a glimpe of the aged face of the little truck's miniature driver: completely unaware of the existence of another car, oblivious to the impending disaster. Later, they painfully climbed out of the crumpled vehicle: a well-weathered farmer and his wife, with a combined height about equal to the driver's own, and sharing a single pair of glasses. Obviously it had been the farmer's turn to drive, but unfortunately it had not been his turn with the glasses.

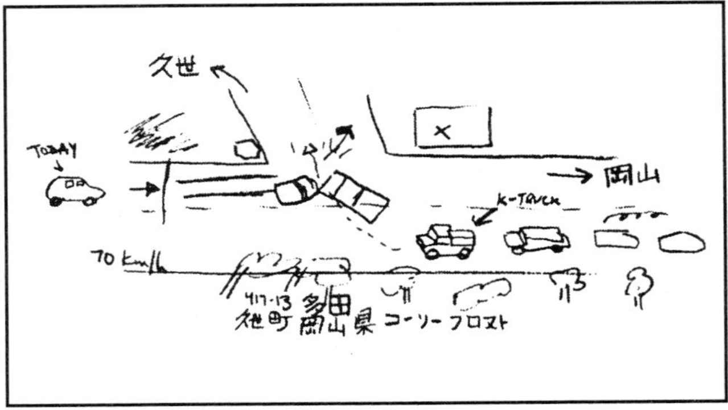

I will not have you suffer any inconvenience.

A car crash is not funny, but it is always extremely ironic. It is therefore an indispensible tool for a writer. It is fairly self-evident that writers are basically stand-up comedians who have failed to be funny. What often goes unnoticed is that people continue to allow writers to exist because humans in general are basically comedians who have failed to be funny. Writers, if they are good, fail even more miserably than most humans do and that is why people like them.

Three

The third crash involved a busload of children, but can not be reproduced here as the rights to the story were not retained by the author.

Can I open my eyes now? The car is heading up, towards the light. Don't look back, says the driver. He is trying to convince us that we have no choice but to continue in a straight line, not looking left or right, to the end of the tunnel and the center of the city. But in truth we can stop the car at any time and get out. At every 500 metres along the tunnel there are emergency telephones.

Four

The fourth crash, like the first, occurred while the driver was in love, but this time the desired person was sitting in the passenger seat. They had been driving all night through America, and the driver was feeling a giddy sort of early-morning happiness; he was in a state that he had never been in before. The vehicle ahead of them, though, was moving despondently. As the driver began to overtake it, the morose vehicle suddenly turned left without signalling. The damage was not serious, but after the crash the door on the passenger side would not open, and the person whom the driver loved was forced to exit the car on the driver's side. The driver had no money for repairs, so from then on anyone who wanted to ride in the car had to enter and exit in this way. Soon after, the loved person stopped riding with the driver altogether, for reasons that the person insisted were unrelated to the accident or the door. In the meantime, the driver's happiness, which had been shattered so perfectly by the accident, did not return at all until six months later, when the door was finally repaired.

A car collision happens randomly and is therefore easy for a writer to implement as a device at any point in a story. Capricious disaster is the trusted accomplice of the psychological realist writer. It is impossible to implement good fortune in the same way, because no one is willing to believe that happiness can be accidental. Everyone is eager to accept disaster, but the twenty-first-century audience will not let a writer get away with arbitrary contrivances if they have positive results. The protagonist must be thwarted: that is the guiding axiom of the Modernist writer. The triumph of Modernist writing is the impressive degree to which disaster is refined, and the hand of fate carefully camouflaged, to the point where no one except the writer is even aware that disaster is taking place at all. A story at this level of refinement will typically end with a sentence such as:

> *As he stared into his coffee cup, Scott knew that in that moment something had changed, that some part of himself had been lost, and he would never get it back.*

or :

> *It was not anything he had said; it was not the flowers wilting in the vase, or the broken vacuum cleaner; it was not any of these things that caused it, but suddenly, the bottom fell out of Julie's world.*

What the Modernist writers understood is that disaster is such a sublime experience that it can happen to anyone, at any time, under any circumstances. In fact, tragedy so often happens to people who are doing nothing more dangerous than idly staring into coffee cups, that this kind of Modernist disaster is often referred to as the bottom-falling-out-of-the-coffee-cup tragedy. Writers who lack such a subtle understanding of disaster, and the author of this story is one example, and F. Scott Fitzgerald is another, must rely on more vulgar kinds of misfortune to end their stories, such as car collisions.

Where will we be when we come out? The driver, who is also the author, is speeding up because the end of the tunnel is visible. He is sad because the car he is driving has a good stereo, but the car of course will have to be scrapped; the material and emotional cost of repair will be more than the author can likely afford. On the stereo a book-on-tape is playing, the only one available at the English bookstore in the city. It is a philosophical thriller. The voice is speaking about a search for Ancient Secrets in the Andes mountains. The voice has just had an astounding revelation, but is now being pursued by cynical, avaricious men with semi-automatic rifles. Then suddenly, just before we emerge, something goes very wrong.

And at that point we are finally ready to begin the story. For although it is perfect, it is often through the crash itself that we see how perfection fails us. The story therefore has no car crashes, no deaths, no irony, no predictable metafiction. By the time the story begins, all of that is over.

The first event of the story is: I open my eyes. Next, everything is blurry. I realize that my glasses are no longer on my face. Next, my neck hurts. Also the windshield is a tangled mass of bright white cracks. There is the gentle noise of a bell emanating from the dashboard, like a metronome. Ding. Ding. Then I hear a voice. It is a familiar voice, the voice of someone I have never seen but who has been speaking to me for a long time. I begin to sing quietly to myself.

I am nice and I am clean;
you are dirty and obscene.
Tonight you'll have a filthy dream,
a dream of blood and gasoline.

I like blood and gasoline,
my heart is like a warm machine.
I like blood and gasoline,
blood and gasoline.

Michel Rivard would like to see the sea

I was born on an island called Prince Edward, that used to be called Île St.Jean, but I frequently left it, because that's what islanders do. They spend their lives going from island to whatever they think is not-island. In my case it was a nearby continent, but I soon found myself on another island, and then yet another.

For example, I now live in Montreal. I moved here over a year ago — my apartment one block east of St.Denis is filled with my bubble. On warm days it spills out the window onto the street. Montrealers recognize my accent as English Canadian, but they often assume that I'm from the rocky Canadian Shield, or the plains, or the mountains. However naïve this may sound, it hurts me. I want them to know that I am distinct too, in my own way. At the same time, I want to have some remote sense of belonging, and once or twice I have lied that I am an apostate Acadian, that my grandparents spoke French, which makes me a recoupable sort of anomaly. I can't go on like this. Sooner or later the decision will have to be made: to which island do I really belong? I'm eighteen.

People are already beginning to ask me questions, trying to get my opinion. The other day the phone rang and someone said she was calling on behalf of someone else and wanted to ask me a series of questions which I could answer with yes, no, or undecided. It seems to be an issue that everyone takes extremely seriously. I know, I said, I've been here a year already, I should have an opinion — but I really don't know what to say. *I live in a bubble in the middle of a city. Sometimes my heart is gray and behind the window I feel boredom falling on the wan faces and under the heavy dragging steps of the passers-by.* I'm eighteen; surely I'll get through this. I have many years ahead of me.

Mireille, the girl I'm in love with at this point in my life although she doesn't know it, comes from another island — several islands, really — in the Gulf of St.Lawrence, north of Prince Edward. *Les Îles-de-la-Madeleine*, the Magdalene Islands: politically and culturally a part of Quebec, but geographically in a world of their own. My own island is small and English; Mireille's island is much smaller and French, which is different after all. While I was first learning French, my thoughts became different and deferred: it always took a bit longer from thought to speech than it had before. At first the time lag was long, suspenseful, with a lot of anxious grappling in between. Then as I improved and the way became familiar, the time lapse gradually shrank. Now, though, I say something, and a fraction of a second later I realize what I've said, because the utterance must first be translated back into my own language before I can understand it completely, and that takes time. First speech, then thought. I am still learning French of course, motivated partly by a longing to make up my mind, and partly by my dreams of Mireille.

In August she sent me a letter from B.C. where she was made an island by the enormity of the continent. *I've finally decided*, she said. *I travelled a little, picked apples for a week, and finally decided not to go home. I want to take life day to day. So I found work in a vegetarian restaurant and lodging with a musician's friends. During two months, I met many great people. Finally, the program offers me a post near Vancouver. So here I am on the bus once again. I will go home in the Fall. I want to welcome you if you will find the time to come to our Islands.*

So here I am on the ferry once again, going to *les Îles-de-la-Madeleine* for only the second time. It's a sunny and chill mid-afternoon in October, 1995, and the water is smooth. We left Souris, P.E.I. thirty minutes ago and we are rounding East Point, but it is impossible to tell which of the undulations in the crumbling red cliff is actually the point. The trip takes five hours. Tomorrow, there is a referendum in which I am expected to vote, but I am still undecided about my answer, yes or no, partly because I don't know how the question is worded. Anyway, at eighteen I am more concerned with very immediate yes or no questions whose wording is largely dictated by hormones. I lean on the railing, watching the line of my island fade like a fog, and watching as *les Îles-de-la-Madeleine* rise from above the horizon, separated from the water by the reflection of the sky, as if they were orbiting satellites. For hundreds of years these islands were as accesible as objects in space, the only contact with the rest of the world being the foreign sailors swept ashore after shipwrecks. Even in this past century, when all the devices of civilization and colonization occasionally broke down, the mail would be sent in a barrel rigged with a sail. The beaches were both immigration center and post office, and you never knew what might wash up when you stepped outside in the morning and looked down the slope of the hill to where the island met the sea. It is a mythical place to me, a miniature kingdom of shipwreck survivors and wandering Acadians, *washed by the gulfstream* like the emerald isle of Stephen Daedalus, with similar questions to ask itself. I have decided to read *Ulysses* on the ferry; I have gotten through about ten pages, although I have already skipped ahead because I wanted to see how it would end.

A picnic appears on a sunny weathered beach, with sea parsley: my first trip to the islands, last summer with my friend Sonia from Montreal. When I became friends with Sonia two years ago I was only sixteen and she was the first real francophone I'd ever met. She gave me a cassette of the songs that meant something to her and I learned the words to Beau Dommage, Harmonium, Paul Piché, and Michel Rivard, who became for me the essence of what it meant to be *Québécois*. Maybe because the meaning was so crystal clear to her, the songs began to mean something to me as well;

at least I thought they did. They all had questions to ask. A song that tries to supply only answers is nothing more than propaganda; art is how people respond when a yes or a no is not enough. But some of the songs, the ones that Sonia thought were most powerful and that I could never remember the words to, asked questions that contained their own implicit answers. For me the songs that resonated most were those in which the meaning was least obvious. The one that's on my mind now is by Michel Rivard. I never really liked the music much; it's a bit elevatorish. But in it there is a kind of blank, a need for an answer, that I can identify with, even if the answers are not at all the answers I expected. The answers only make sense if I try to compose a suitable question to go with the song. And the obvious question I always come up with — I don't really understand why someone would ask it — is: would you like to see to the sea? When I ask myself this question, I realize I have an ambiguous relationship to the ocean.

The ocean, for me, represents freedom, distance, isolation, destiny, eternity. Strange words to associate when you think about it, especially isolation and freedom. Perhaps for some people, like Sonia, who grew up knowing that she belonged to Quebec and that Quebec belonged to her, freedom might mean finding a way to isolate your community. But for Mireille and the rest of the Madelinots, who have always had isolation in abundance, it is mainly a question of association. And for me too.

One must believe that we become habituated, that we take the taste for that. So here I am on the bus once again. I am coming back from Nelson where I passed a marvelous week, high in the mountains. I am fasting since seven days. And you? Do you pass a good year in Montréal?

I don't see the minke whales now but on the ferry last summer Sonia and I watched them dip and roll beside the boat like a hand held palm down out a car window. The day after we arrived at Cap-aux-Meules we met Sylvain, who makes shoes, and the four of us went to the beach. I thought or hoped at the time that Mireille and Sylvain were just good friends. Or possibly family. There was something about their innocence and openness that made me believe that, but also something about how Mireille smiled at me that made me want to believe it. And when they got naked and jumped into the frothy waves in chilly June I stripped too and splashed into *the scrotumtightening sea*. Even on the south shore of Île-du-Havre-Aubert, the gulf was crisp with melted ice. But I surprised myself, and I was exhilarated, because I would never have done that on my own island. I wasn't self-conscious even staggering out of the seaweed on to the soft beach in the wind, my frozen penis growing warm in the sun. We all towelled off shivering and laughing, and when the ocean evaporated from my skin I felt like I was breathing for the first time. The air tasted different, salty. Then along the sand talking and sinking our feet into invisible holes, very happy, and my life was as hard to imagine as that beach covered in snow. In French the possibility of speech overwhelmed me as if it were a new idea — there was a different word for everything. The sun was outshone by the warmth I felt from Mireille. How the day felt open. I thought, that's how it is here. A picnic on a sunny weathered beach with sea parsley.

I had met Mireille once before — in Montreal that spring. She was there to greet Sonia on our return from a long voyage with other young bilingual Canadians, thanks to one of Trudeau's programs. At that point I had not yet lived in Montreal and did not even know it that well, but I sang happily along with "*Tous les Palmiers*" by Beau Dommage as we touched down.

Sonia introduced me to her friend from *les Îles-de-la-Madeleine*. At that moment I realized for the first time that I was thinking in French, that I had been for months. Mireille touched my arm like an embrace; she said we were kin — both islanders. In her words isolation seemed so intimate. It could be freedom, intimacy, hardship, and fear all at once. Although my French was still not refined enough to recognize her Acadian accent, she asked if I was francophone or anglophone and in my joy I wanted to take her hand, run away and prolong the confusion. With my cartoon-like understanding of the world I wanted to rush out to a *cabane à sucre*, put on more fashionable clothes, and eat *pâté chinois*. I wanted to drink wine with my meals and sing about wanting to see the sea.

I hope that all goes well for you.

I hope that you are happy.

Prends soin de toi!

Sonia and Mireille and Sylvain and I drove to the alabaster cliffs of Le Bassin and stood staring west at the *rocher du corps mort* on the horizon — strange and unidentifiable at first as though it could be just a speck of dirt in your eye, but then becoming more solid, establishing its own claim on reality and finally growing so that it dominated the entire seascape and we could see the individual clefts in its huge cliff face, the waves crashing on its rocks. We ate on the beach and added sea parsley to our salad; we made a bonfire and played charades for an hour, then walked along the dunes to see the windmill on its vertical axis, a giant eggbeater.

The night was devoid of cities and much darker, although the sand was glowing with a dim golden light stored up through the day. The stars did cartwheels through the sky as we shuffled along the beach — thousands of stars that I could never have seen in the city. We walked along a thin strip of sand with the churning ocean on one side as regular and vital as blood, and the freshwater pond on the other as quiet as the surface of an eye. Then we could hear it, when we could still only see three red lights in a vertical line, a dull rhythmic sound like a monolithic heartbeat or the first few turns of a propeller. When we could see it we were already so close that I wanted to drop to my knees to avoid the two enormous white arms of the ellipse whipping by so irresistibly, high above our heads. I could tell the others were intimidated as well. Sylvain and Mireille were clinging to one other. Sylvain said something to me that I didn't understand, some expression that I had never learned. Mireille was looking past the windmill, to the water. I thought I felt the ground under the ocean shake, as if the whole earth were on the same axis as that blade.

I always have the taste to travel, she says in her letter. *I would like to go to Central America and to South America. I want to learn Spanish. I would also like to go live with my friends. And sometimes I have 'mal du pays.' I miss the sea, and also Sylvain. As you can notice, I have lots of questions in my head.*

Now the light is already growing dim and Île D'Entrée is just visible — the only island not joined to the others by sand dunes, with its self-ostracized population of anglophones. It is already dark when the boat arrives. Mireille meets me on the pier with her brother.

In order to keep living in a meaningful way people have to constantly ask themselves questions. Some people feel the need to constantly ask other people questions as well. Fortunately these questions can usually be answered with yes or no. Are you hungry? Would you like another piece? Isn't that the most gorgeous sunset you've ever seen? Is this seat taken? Are you paying more for your heating than you would like? Have you ever had sexual relations with that woman? Are these your shoes? Am I speaking to Mr. Michel Rivard? Can you give me some change for food not alcohol? Moving? Did you know about the activities of the para-military group connected to your government? Do you accept Jesus as your saviour? Can I help you? Would you like to see the sea, swollen with the sun, become a jewel as big as the earth?

What we have is a binary system. Although choosing the right answer is extremely important, our fears can be allayed by the knowledge that the answer is always either yes or no — on or off — the only other option being no answer or empty set, which is used in cases where the question was only rhetorical. The answers to the questions above, for example, are yes, yes, no, yes, yes, yes, no, no, yes, yes, no, no, no, and I'm not sure if that applies to me. As easy as it is to decide on an answer, it is extremely difficult to decide on the wording of the question, which is what ultimately dictates what the answer will be, since each yes answer is also, at the same time, a no answer to that question's inverse twin. Aren't you Michel Rivard? Yes, I am not Michel Rivard.

Mireille's brother Jean-Denis is married to Marinalva who is from Brazil but lives on the Islands now with her Madelinot husband. She wears a small pink rose in her hair. We stay in their farmhouse on a hill on Île-du-Havre-aux-Maisons. They have spent the day taking in the last of the carrots and zucchini from the garden. In the winter, when vegetables are expensive on the Islands, they will store the carrots and potatoes in a box of dirt in the basement.

At night after blackberry crumble and herbal tea, after Mireille and I have climbed the narrow steps whose treads are as smooth as seashells, she turns and presents me with another question. It will be maybe cold in that room, she says. Do you want to sleep in my bed? *would I yes to say yes and first I wanted to put my arms around her yes and draw her down to me so she could feel my breast all wildflower perfume yes and my heart was going like mad and I wanted to say yes I wanted yes to say yes,* except I don't know exactly what it will mean if I say yes. The question is too ambiguous. I want to say yes so badly that I am petrified of what the consequences may be if I have misunderstood, and I have to say no. My bed is old and comfortable, high off the ground and covered with hand-made quilts, but it is cold.

The next day we are all going to the regional high school to vote but first Sylvain and Mireille and I are driving to the highest point in the islands for an overview. The way Sylvain talks about independence is the way he talks about making shoes. I just want to make something, he says in his little grey Chevette on the way up the hill. Something I can say I made myself. He shifts gears and the road turns to dirt so we roll up the windows. I just want to live here on these little islands and make shoes. I can feel the leather; with my hands I can tell the quality of it. I know where it comes from: right here on the Islands. And it is something useful. I believe that we must try to be self-sufficient like any nation.

It is impossible to hear what Mireille is saying in the back seat because of the engine and wind so she sits back while he talks. Then Sylvain reaches down — his eyes just clearing the beat-up dash to peer through the wind and dust — and pulls off one shoe and hands it to his passenger, saying, I grew up here, just like Mireille. I could go live in Montreal, but if I can stay here and make things like that and breathe the ocean I know I will be happy. I have much respect for those who live where they belong. Some people live here for maybe three months of the year or just visit and then leave in the winter. I wouldn't do that. Mireille, too, she will come back.

We park the little car with its plaid seats at the end of the path and race each other up the slope, diving into pools of mustard and daisies, Queen Anne's lace and the devil's paintbrushes. It is higher than it looks and our muscles are drenched at the end. We hold hands like paper dolls. At the top loitering around the massive base of the radio tower, the sky is staring at itself in the grey sea. Our words are blown away and down the slopes, across the tops of spruce trees dwarfed by weather, past the clusters of jelly-bean wooden houses on the shore and along miles of shifting dunes to the north and south. Beyond that the water stretches away like a Euclidean plane dotted with sheep. There are only faint maritime clouds on the horizon. Sylvain's arm is around Mireille. Then she steps away from him trailing fingers and comes over to me, reaches up and kisses me. Takes my hand. I must seem lonely. And the corner of my sight encompasses her tiny isolated smile as she closes her eyes. I taste the ocean in the air around her. My fingers and my lips are aware of it, a peculiar sensation I can't identify. It's a scent that I know is not mine, and it makes me envious. *And I wanted to put the rose in my hair like the Brazilian girls used or shall I wear a red yes and how she kissed me under the radio tower and I thought well as well me as him and then I wanted to ask her with my eyes and I wanted to be asked—*

And all around us is a gulf — a huge wide gulf that shares its blood with oceans, between our two islands. I ask myself if I could live here in this insular world, each year for maybe three months, or just visit? I'm eighteen; sometimes my heart is grey, but I know I'll get through this if you ask me the right question. I know I will be happy. If only I am asked the right question, then I know exactly what my answer will be. It will be *yes I would like to see the sea and her silver beaches and her proud white cliffs in the wind. I would like to see the sea and her moon-birds and her fog-horses and her flying fish. I would like to see the sea when she is a mirror where woolen clouds pass without seeing themselves. I would like to see the sea, and dance with her, to defy death.* But the words of the song are garbled in my language; the texture of the sentences is different. It is exactly as if the words were submerged, as if I were looking down at them through a layer of briny water. There is ocean between us, separating me from the words, but this does not necessarily mean that the words are submerged. It is entirely possible, I suppose, that it's me.

Being, with Americans

New York! says the head animator of the immersion program. I read a novel that said everyone should live in New York at least once in their life. I don't think I read that one, I tell her. The statue of liberty you sent me is two inches tall, and its face is all puffy. Turn the page when you hear Tinkerbell's wings jingle like this:

I arrive at the envelope factory early, with the morning sun sluicing in broad ribbons between the warehouses, where the bricks in the road were once ballast in emigrant ships. Under the bridge it is raining fat drops of dirty water that glitter like spangles in the sun. Up the street the Jehovah's Witlesses oversee the neighbourhood from their watchtower made of — I believe — plywood. Bud's doorbell doesn't work, so I call his shoe-phone. I guess being a Canadian in New York is pretty uncool, I say to Bud. Everybody in New York is uncool, he says, unless they're black.

Bud is a full-time studio engineer and DJ, part-time scoundrel, with interest in a lust-for-life mutual fund. Which part of Life, Liberty, and the pursuit of Happiness didn't you understand? he wants to know. It's hard to argue with his *carpe-diem* philosophy and he knows it. Luckily, my phone receives email, mostly from you, and I send some to you too. *I got the underwear yesterday, thanks for sending them. I love it that you love potatoes.*

Hello. A forest fire near James Bay has blanketed Ottawa, Montreal, and even Toronto with a cloud of ash. That's why the sun is orange and faint like that. Apocalyptic, isn't it? When the slightly obese man at the Social Security office sees my passport he says, You the one who's been making the sky all funny? Bud has already pointed out to me, quite reasonably, that I shouldn't base my impressions of a whole country on one visit to a Roy Rogers on the State Thruway. *Last night a guy at the* yakitori *pulled down his pants at the bar and lit his pubic hair on fire. Meg said that when you smell burning pubes you get three wishes.*

These are exciting times, but confusing times, says the foreign student counsellor at the orientation session. I am excited at first, but then confused. It turns out he is only talking about visa procedures. The IAP-66 you are all familiar with — he holds up a pink slip of paper — is from now on going to be called the DS-2019 — dramatic pause — *but it's exactly the same document*. Gasps, rustling of papers as some students take out their documents and look them over with newfound anxiety. Let's take a break, says the counsellor. I'm going to lead you all in trying to touch the ceiling.

Americans write the date differently from every other culture in the world, the counsellor tells us. Don't ask me why! He writes it on the board as he says it: MM, DD, YYYY. Don't ask me why! He encourages us to integrate ourselves into American society. Your life in America is not just about being in class and reading books, he informs us. It's also about being with Americans.

How was your orientation session? It was fascinating. I learned about being with Americans, and about dating, American-style.

Cate is waiting next to William Shakespeare. I thought I'd be early, but she's been there five minutes already (five *New York* minutes, that is). There is ice cream nearby; the sun is practically working up a saxophone solo; the park is cluttered with rollerbladers, lunatics, and underwear models, all dripping with stinky beauty. I know she would rather be in the West Bank.

Hunting for an apartment in New York is one of the great epic struggles of our times, you say. *I feel stressed just knowing you.* When I tell Cate what I expect from my ideal apartment, she tells me to write it down and sell it as pornography. Let the record show that my fantasies have been duly crushed like so many Bushwick cockroaches. I thought we would have lunner together (it's not quite lunch, not quite dinner). Instead I am left to my own devices. The woman at Columbus Circle whom I ask for a tuna sandwich is jumping up and down, and continues jumping, knees locked together, while she makes my sandwich, wraps it, hands it to me, and takes my money. "I have to go to the bathroom," she explains. "Well," I say, taking my change. "Good luck."

That night I meet up with Jessie and her new boyfriend at a sake bar in the East Village. I ask directions of the many young white people in tight t-shirts, but they don't know anything. Finally, after some cell-phone calls for clarification, I find them and we have $6 cups of sake and $4 bowls of edamame. On the subway are posters asking us to embrace the future, in Spanish. The city has a touch of post-traumatic stress disorder. *Life doesn't just go on forever, you know. Enjoy your banana-free day.*

As I cross the bridge on the Q, the skyscrapers shift and move around the conspicuously empty center. First the demolition in July 1972 of the Pruitt-Igoe housing development in St. Louis, and now this. I can live in the oxygen-rich air of aesthetic revolution, no problem, but the idea looms that there are good deals on nuclear weapons out there, if you know where to look. *Who will do the swimming in this relationship? I'll do the swimming and the piano playing, if you'll make the spicy noodles and the ironic dance moves.*

I have to leave the very next day. I can't tell you which highway to take, says the African-American driver of the paper-shredding truck, but I can give you its initials. He is dressed head to toe in white hooded coveralls, shoes covered in white slippers, wearing a mask and dark glasses. He may not be African-American.

I have never felt more alive than this, crossing the steel-blue bridge on a Tuesday morning in the middle of the year. I shout a meaningless euphoric syllable, a barbaric yawp that floats out over the river and hopefully reaches the roofs of Alphabet City. *I heart*

NY. I also heart email and bagels and Pingu.

There may very well have been times when I felt *equally* as alive. It's hard to measure these things. One evening in Nara stands out in my mind, visiting the giant Buddha and watching the sun set from a wooden bench. When Kathleen had written that story with the words "I can't believe this is my life," which caused me so much agony. Early AM with Joanne, riding in the back of the tilted pick-up across the dusty *sertão*. May 8th, 1991, when we drove across the country with Paul ("Sits With Luggage") in the back seat. Seth ("Worries About Tires") and I ("Analyzes Self") declared it New Year's Day. Hiking to Cape Split, when we built a human pyramid on the grass near the cliff. I'm the only one not in the picture, because I was learning to take photographs. Feeling indiscriminately in love. I wish I had never aspired to be a photographer. It's obviously not an exact science. *Thank-you for sending me the picture of a storefront that said "Goodbye Modernism." Don't worry, by the way. I don't think you are a Modernist. I was just kidding.*

The statue of liberty has grown to six inches in two days. I have to remind myself that that is Manhattan. Toronto is often disguised as New York in movies; how can I be sure that's not going on here? What else could explain how easily I found an apartment? Maybe hundreds of corpulent men in orange vests scurry to set up graffiti-covered facades and strew garbage everywhere I go. The agile Chicana lover of poetry tells me, anyone who lives here has to realize sooner or later that they are not the star of the movie. Even if you are shooting a movie and you're the star. It is perhaps New York's biggest contribution to civilization. Twelve million stories in the naked city; adding two more is perhaps excessive — let's try one. *Others have loved before us, I know we are not new.* That's what Lenny says. *I'm looking at all of this with love and difficulty.*

Knowledge Mints

I want to thank Andy Brown, not only for coaxing me to finish this book, and not only for investing his time and energy into its editing and design with basically little hope of reward or recognition, and not only for not complaining when I left four winter tires on his balcony and cross-country skis in his closet, and not only for his unceasing dedication to making conundrum press into a new publishing nexus for Montreal writers — one that accomodates and encourages a wider range of interests and ambitions including comix and spoken word — but also for being a thoroughly decent fellow whom everyone likes and whom no one, it seems to me, thanks or acknowledges enough. I want to thank Marc Bell for drawing some devices for me. I would like to acknowledge and thank the Canada Council for the assistance they've given me and also that given to small presses such as conundrum. I want to thank, specifically among my many editors, the members of a writing group to which I once belonged, who were the first to read some of these stories — namely, Dana Bath, Francesca Lodico, Liane Keightley, and Taien Ng-Chan, and I want to especially thank Catherine Kidd, Patchen Barss, Maeve Haldane, and Cynthia Quarrie, for criticism and care. Here's to purity, beat poets, war-queens, and the moon. Affectionate thanks go to all the other constituents of the particular Montreal subculture of which I have been a part, writers and performers and artists and active audience, for their enthusiasm and brilliance. I want to thank my family in the Maritimes, which is sometimes too far away, for their unconditional love and support.

My Own Devices

Acknowledgements are due to the Tokyo death-metal band Neverfear, to Aeroflot, to Vladimir Propp, to Canada World Youth, to Wim Wenders, to David Lynch, to Julio Cortázar, to Jonathan Swift, to Bell Canada, to J.G. Ballard and to David Cronenberg, to Michel Rivard and to Beau Dommage, to James Joyce, to Kenji Kawakami, to Alfred Lord Tennyson, to Emily Dickinson, to Kathy Acker, to Gail Scott, to Marcel Proust, to Walter Benjamin, to Cibo Matto, and to Commodore. That, really, is just a sampling. I want to thank George Fogarasi for allowing me to quote his essay "All that is Soridu Melts into Kitty," which can be found at www.ctheory.net, as can "A l'Ombre du Millénaire..." by Jean Baudrillard, whom I also thank although he never said I could quote him. Octavio Paz and Roland Barthes are dead, so I acknowledge them but do I need to thank them? What about Pizzicato Five? They are famous pop stars, which is as good as being dead. I acknowledge that the world is wide and complicated and that there is a lot I don't know or am only guessing at.

Finally, here is a list, compiled using rigidly stochastic principles and no doubt suffering from numerous serious and embarassing accidental omissions, of the people from whom I have borrowed bits of identity and history to make these stories, or who were on my mind when I wrote them. Some play significant parts in my emotional well-being (or emotional tumult, as the case may be), and they know who they are. Some of them just happened to be passing by. See how many characters in the stories you can match to the real people below!! Andy, Robbie, Lisa, Ben, Sylvie, Patchen, Heather, Meredith, Peter, Lorne, Anne, Kathleen, Sara, Theresa, Joanne, David, Sonia, Noaldo, JoséArmando, Laerte, Annie, Sylvain, Maeve, Catherine, Trish, Dana, Jack, Kathy, Dave, Esme, Takeshi, Tsuboi-san, Maeda-san, Michi, Ray, Komoto-san, Cedar, John, Dilli, Irina, Pascale, Roberto, Ellen, Justin, Jennifer, Raina, Patti, and Cynthia. *Terima kasih.*

Left to my own devices

The story of the year

We settled this time on Boulevard St. Laurent, the Greenwich of Montreal — the zero-degrees-longitude where east and west hemispheres divide, street numbers climbing from one in both directions. In our neighbourhood between Fairmount and St. Viateur the Indian restaurants cluster mainly on the east side, while on the west there are a couple of Italian groceries, a Portuguese restaurant, and a trendy café serving coffee and chocolate, western hemisphere treasures. And we too are perched on the west side of the street, as far east as we can get without being in the East, and as we look across the Boulevard from our balcony, a Japanese restaurant looks back at us from the other side.

Just in front of the balcony we have the shade of a single tree. It's not a very big tree, not really tall enough to give shade, but with enough leaves at least to rustle in the wind and give an illusory relief from the heat in the summer, a bit of greenery to lessen the smoggy grey pallor of the warehouses on either side. That's what I thought when we moved in last September, when there were still leaves on it, but now that we are once again January, in the cold limbo between the Western New Year and the Chinese New Year, it's hard to imagine that brittle, barren tree giving relief from anything. The street is frozen; it has been coated with rain that freezes and unfreezes and freezes again, hovering right around that zero-degree mark, hesitating between one side and the other. We are all unsure of our footing. The sidewalks are out-of-bounds, like ice-covered beaches along this boulevard-*fleuve*, blurring the boundary between the continent and the ocean. It's been like that for several days now.

We are watching the newscast that people are watching all across the country, but the images on the screen are pictures of here: a few blocks away, a few kilometres away. The story of the year is the weather. Southern Quebec and northern New England are paralyzed, shot with a super-villain's Freeze Ray. The surface of everything is suddenly untouchable behind inches of ice, kept at a distance like a bug in amber or a museum display under glass. Peter Mansbridge on the CBC, his expression serious-but-just-as-amazed-as-you-are, gives us the unbelievable details: bridges, highways, whole towns shut down; the army being called in — uselessly, ridiculously; ice shearing off skyscrapers in massive lethal sheets; people actually killed by falling branches. He already has a logo above his left shoulder, and there are epithets: "Icy Grip", "Deep Freeze". Some other things did happen today, he informs us, but we'll get to that later.

Then, while we are watching an image of trees crashing onto electrical lines, the picture folds up and collapses into a sharp, tiny point of light, drawing everything into it like a black hole, which quickly fades and disappears. All the lights go out, the fridge stops humming. We don't know where the matches are. I feel my way to the kitchen window at the back of the apartment, looking out over the west: no points of light, no fridges humming. The sky, though, is extremely bright and orange, as if a great fire were raging a few blocks away. I am suddenly more alarmed. Turning, I look down the long corridor and out the windows at the front, across the Main. In the east, in the loft across the street, the lights are still on. Kathleen is standing at the window, silhouetted against the orange glow of the street. I go and stand next to her and gaze across the street at the sushi bar, feeling acutely the separation of worlds. Power, no power. And then, as soon as this idea has had time to sink in, the lights on the other side blink out as well.

Wide-scale failure of devices

The first evening without power was romantic and fun, I admit. We played Scrabble in the light of six candles stuck crookedly into empty wine bottles; I went out for pizza which we ate in bed, in the dark (it came with free ice-cold beverages). That night we piled every blanket on the bed, and extra coats as well, and burrowed underneath. I was reminded of nights on the other side, in the little unheated Japanese house, when I would wake up in the morning and the thermometer on the kerosene heater would read zero, and I would reach a timid unprotected toe out from the end of the futon to touch the on button.

We spent a couple of days coming to the obvious realization that all the central objects of our lives require electricity. I had to consciously remind myself, over and over, that not only was it impossible to do any writing on my computer, but I couldn't even check my email. In fact, all the activities I could think of as alternatives to our normal routine proved also impossible. One of my first ideas was to invite people over, to sit around in the candlelight and drink tea — I associate candles with tea. But we have no way of making tea. For some reason I turned to tea when I realized that I would have no coffee at home. I finally went out and walked until I found a café with power, to imbibe my caffeine for the day, and Seth met me there. He made fun of me, suggesting that if tea could not be made then we would simply have to have *herbal* tea. I tried to think of foods to prepare that did not need cooking and I had settled on humus until I remembered that I would need the blender. The only warm thing we ate was bagels and cream cheese, because we could get them fresh from the bagel bakery's wood-fired oven at any time of day — the bagels, despite weather of any kind, must go on. I don't know how often I thought of renting movies for the evening. I couldn't even return the movie we had rented the night before, because the VCR would not eject it without power. Everything was frozen.

Most of our devices had become useless. There was no instantaneous communication because our telephone is of the kind that needs to be plugged in. There was no way to tell time because all the clocks also require AC. There was music, however; we spent hours playing the game where you take turns singing Beatles songs, or where you sing songs containing questions. Not everything was inoperative, though: our books worked, of course, with the interface of a candle, including the dictionary. We spent some time reading to one another. Device: the word comes from the Middle French *division* and the Old French *deviser* which means "to divide, to regulate, to tell." To divide, like drawing a line down the middle of a globe, or separating a year into days or a country into smaller countries. To tell, like creating a story. The first meaning is "something devised". (Devise: to form in the mind by new combinations or applications of ideas or principles. To invent, conceive, bring about.) It can be a plan, a procedure, or a technique. It can be a scheme to deceive, or it can be something fanciful, elaborate or intricate in design. It is often something (for example, a figure of speech) in a literary work designed to achieve an artistic effect. It can be any equipment or mechanism designed to serve a specific purpose. Another meaning is "an emblematic design, as in heraldry": an icon, especially one that identifies a name. ("The device of the Frost clan.") And finally, a third meaning is "inclination, desire", as in "left to my own devices", which is exactly how we described ourselves in the absence of power.

Reduced to abstract sculptures of plastic and silicon, our devices seemed not less attractive to me but more interesting, as I began to regard them in terms of aesthetics rather than function. Their sudden uselessness made them curious objects, as though the most irresistible attraction of a device lies in its very superfluousness and impracticality. The most desirable device is that which is beyond the realm of the sensible or the easily comprehendible. This is the fundamental paradox of *chindogu* ("an odd or distorted tool"). *Chindogu* are inventions that seem like they're going to make life a lot easier, but don't. Shining examples are tiny dusters for a cat's paws, a fish face cover (to avoid having to look into its lifeless eyes), umbrellas for one's shoes, or a chin-operated light switch. All of these devices exist; it seems as though simply imagining a device may be enough to guarantee its eventual production. By the same token, the invention of a fictional website (for example, www.coreyfrost.com) is an exercise in contradiction and/or futility, since either a) it already exists somewhere among the millions of real pages available, or b) the naming of an imaginary website will create an irresistible impulse for someone to produce a "real life" version with that name, because the opportunity for profit exists in controlling the gap between reality and people's imaginings and desires. The only way to create true fiction, then, is to keep it secret.

We spent a few nights in utter devicelessness, and we probably could have survived quite well for weeks, because we are hardy Canadians to whom it occurs naturally to wear a toque indoors. Nevertheless, I won't say we were disappointed when Jason and Evelyn dropped by and invited us over. We were just sitting down to a dinner of cold congealed pizza and melting ice cream. Their apartment is only a few blocks away to the east, and they have no electricity either, but there is gas heat and a gas-powered cooking stove. We've come for supper bearing semi-thawed chili, but it looks like we may stay and be warm for a night, for a change. Kathleen is in favour of abandoning the winter survival camp immediately and staying on their living room hide-a-bed until power is restored. The idea is attractive to me too, but I argue with her quietly that perhaps Jason and Evelyn don't want storm refugees in their three-and-a-half apartment. Really, though, I just can't help feeling that evacuation means giving up, failing to accept the challenge that fate has dealt us. We have been getting along fine, the two of us, in our frigid apartment. I want to see this as an opportunity to transcend ourselves. I don't say that, though, because even to me it sounds melodramatic and corny, and I know she would find it risible. I desperately love her, but we have reached a point in our relationship where neither of us has much patience or indulgence left for the other. "Well, you can go home if you want. I'm staying here," she says. My arguments for mutual independence backfire in situations like this, those times when I *do* want us to depend on each other. Until the storm, I had almost forgotten how much I do want that, sometimes.

Corey Frost:
Gained a year of life in the Ice Storm of '98

There is really no argument to be made, of course, and in the end we decide to stay, at least for the night. We sit at the melamine kitchen table, drinking wine and talking about the weather, our faces illuminated by the flickering light from a pewter candelabra. The individual flames are mirrored in my glasses, and when Jason and then Kathleen remove their contacts and put on glasses I can see the lights dancing in front of their eyes too. Jason has a battery-powered transistor radio, which reminds me of camping trips in the seventies, and we listen to the latest news on the state of the city. The Metro is closed down, the mountain is off-limits because of the danger of falling trees, and since the water treatment plants aren't operational we are advised to boil water before drinking it, which is fine if you have a gas stove. We are also told that the Montreal Canadiens game has been cancelled, and I file this away as a perfect illustration of the word "ironic" — apparently the Molson Centre is unable to make ice. Each of us has an anecdote to contribute to our collective appreciation of how extraordinary the situation is. Jason talks about visiting Warshaws where there was a run on candles, people racing each other to grab the last few boxes. Stories of price-gouging and hoarding are going around, although they don't get the same publicity as the televised stories of altruistic volunteers. It's hard to say which kind of report is more common or more accurate, but still we tell ourselves that in crisis we are better humans, not worse, because we suppose that believing it will make it true.

Two days ago, before they closed the university, I was in a poetry class when there was a knock on the door and a young man came in to inform us that, "A state of emergency has been declared." He was only about twenty years old, earnest, kempt, and I thought to myself, surely we are not expected to take this seriously. Some of the students in the class groaned in exasperation or anger, as if it were someone's fault that they had not been able to have a hot shower that morning. When I relate this story, Evelyn comments on how Canadians are so invested in a discourse of weather control — meteorology is like a national religion, she says — that anger is inevitable when the weather acts uncontrollably.

Both Evelyn and Jason are grad students, happy for any opportunity to apply Deleuze or Foucault to the world around them, and soon we are analyzing the TV coverage of the Storm of the Century. We agree that it would not likely have been awarded that title if people weren't already preoccupied with the end of the millennium, the supposedly imminent Y2K catastrophe and other imagined apocalypses. Furthermore, although none of us believe that the millennium signifies anything other than the whim of a long-dead calendar-devising pope, it is possible that apocalyptic visions can be self-fulfilling prophecies. From there the conversation turns, somehow, to talk-shows — specifically, the kind that exploit the misery and failures of the participants, who always seem eager to have their trauma summarized in a caption under their name on the screen. We debate whether the ice storm represents a significant enough hardship that it could be parlayed into an appearance on Jerry Springer. Some kind of lewd behaviour or depravity would have to be added, Jason observes. "I had sex with my brother during a blackout," suggests Evelyn. "I stabbed my husband with an icicle," adds Kathleen.

We are getting ready to go to bed, brushing our teeth with borrowed toothpaste, when the power comes back on. We call around to some of our other friends and get conflicting reports: the power is on all the way up one street, but just a block away it is off. There are too many lines down, wires snapped; it's impossible to guess whether we have power at home, so I volunteer to walk over and see. If it's still off, I'll come back. If it's on, I'll call, I tell Kathleen. And I think to myself, then you can come home too, and it will be just the two of us again. She doesn't say she'll come home, though. She just says, "Call."

As I am wrapping my neck in a scarf, I remember to tell Jason and Evelyn about the birthday party I am planning for myself in a couple of weeks.

"How old will you be?" asks Evelyn.

"Twenty-seven," I reply. It seems like a high number, but I've reconciled myself to it by now. For a while, unexpectedly, the number had made me fear getting old. I found it disagreeable that my twenties were passing so quickly, and I avoided thinking about it, but now I am somewhat nonchalant. Twenty-seven.

I'm thinking this when Kathleen interrupts: "No, you won't."

"What?"

"You won't be turning twenty-seven."

At first I think she is just being antagonistic, and I am slightly annoyed that she thinks I could get my own age wrong. "Yes, I will," I say, matter-of-factly.

"How old are you now?" she quizzes me.

"Twenty-six. Aren't I?"

"What year were you born?"

"1972."

She is right, of course; I'm capable of doing the calculation myself. Evelyn finds it funny, but Kathleen creases her brow as if I was being dumb on purpose, playing the absent-minded eccentric. The mistake embarrasses and puzzles me a bit, but at the same time, as I step onto the smooth, crystallized street, suddenly a year younger than I thought I was, how can I not feel quietly euphoric?

Crossing the bar

Spending the evening in a candle-lit apartment with a glass of wine in my hand, free of options or obligations, has been a pleasure, but once the bright incandescent lights come on again I am glad to leave, glad to be walking by myself along the meridian in the middle of Boulevard St. Joseph. There are no cars on the road, no people on the sidewalks, and the trees are gleaming glass chimes that strike up a chorus of creaking and crackling whenever there is a gust of wind. As I start to walk west what amazes me most, however, is the sky. It must be about ten o'clock, but it is almost as bright as any stormy winter afternoon, perhaps because the ice crystals in the air reflect the distant street lights a million different ways and cast a diffuse orange glow over the city. It also occurs to me that maybe the sky is often like that, and if everyone would just turn off their lights at once we would see it. In the park on the corner of St. Laurent, I stop to admire the imposing facade on the east side. I often walk past this church, but I have never seen it like this: frosted like a giant cake, sleeping restlessly at the edge of the park, cutting crooked shapes into the amber sky. The surreal nocturnal daylight only adds to the feeling I have that I am walking in a segment of time that doesn't belong to me. I have a whole year ahead of me that I didn't expect to have, as if I had come across it abandoned on the sidewalk.

I do not understand how I lost track of the years I've spent on earth. It's just a memory lapse, a mathematical blunder, but I still find myself wondering what to do with the extra time. When Western Europe switched from the Julian calendar to the Gregorian calendar in 1572, ten days were dropped from the year. Everyone suddenly found themselves ten days older without any memory of that time, because it never happened. I find that miniscule gap in history worrisome, because a lot can happen in ten days. Flying west across the international date line has a similar effect; a whole day is suddenly lost to you in the blink of an eye, although the loss will be made up when you fly back across the line, if you ever do. My situation may be just an illusion caused by my own miscalculation, but those other temporal anomalies are no less illusions. The tangible result is that my future suddenly feels more spacious, as if I had accidentally kicked a hole in the wall of the past and found a spare room hidden there.

I fall down a couple of times crossing the park, and it's so tricky getting back up that I find it easier just to crawl. If those ten days had not disappeared from 1572, would the same events have happened? Somehow it makes me nervous to ponder that question. We like to think we understand the story of the past, what happened in all those previous centuries, so that we can make sense of what is happening now, and feel better about not knowing what will happen next. The main effect of reading a story, though, is that you begin to expect an ending, and with history the ending may never come, or if it does we will not be around to see it — we will never know how it all works out, there will never be any *denouement*. History just goes on as long as you are inclined and able to follow it, and the climax never comes, except at your death. We need stories for this reason, so that we can witness an ending before we experience it for ourselves.

Next to the park is St. Laurent, and although I see lights on this side of the street, on our side it seems like the power is still out. I walk in the street because its crusty slush is easier to navigate than the glassy surface of the sidewalk. When I was quite young, I remember clearly, I loved to put on my snowsuit and lie down in a snow bank with my eyes closed. I liked its crisp embrace, the way it wrapped around my limbs. My mother told me not to do it — she was afraid I would fall asleep there and wake up dead — but she didn't know that I did it because it felt like death, or what I imagined death would be, sinking beneath the surface of the snow. I had many theories of death at that age, in my complete ignorance of the topic: I imagined that it might come suddenly, at any moment, and I tried to predict its arrival. I would say to myself, if I eat that peanut instead of this one, I will die. If I don't get into bed before my mother turns off the light, I will die. Riding in the car, I would think, "If we pass that red truck," or "As soon as we cross that bridge." At the ordained moment, once the boundary had been crossed, I supposed a change would occur. I would immediately find myself in another place, larger than this world and empty. I had these ideas because I so little understood what death meant, but still, I don't understand it any better now than I did then.

When I arrive back at our apartment, there are no lights anywhere along our block. Something else is different too, something is missing, but it doesn't register at first. I cross the street, unlock the door, and go up the stairs which are covered in gravel from dirty boots. Upstairs it is dark — although there is enough light for me to find my way around — and cold — although warm compared to a typical January in Montreal. For a few moments I stand at the top of the stairs, wondering what to do next. I could go back to the warm apartment and the warm bed with the warm body waiting for me only a few blocks away, but I feel like I should uncover some purpose to this visit by doing something while I am here. Ignoring the mess my boots are making, I walk into the bedroom and let myself fall on the pile of blankets, still wearing my parka and scarf and hat. I close my eyes. It's comfortable lying there, and I consider staying and drifting off to sleep. I've got a whole year ahead of me, with inclination or desire as my only guides.

It is only later, when I leave the dark room and step back onto the sidewalk, that I realize our tree has fallen down. The trunk is completely split, the stump is a bouquet of broad splinters as tall as I am, and the branches are lying on the ground amid branch-shaped fingers of ice. Something gained, something lost. The next day the ice storm is over and we move back into our loft apartment, but as the winter gets colder we realize how difficult it is to heat. We are never warm enough, and when the temperature rises to zero degrees we are grateful.

Although not the last poem written by Tennyson, "Crossing the Bar" is, at his request, the final poem in all collections of his work.

Sasu o wataru

(Crossing the Bar)

Nichibotsu to yuugata no hoshi to
  hakkiri shita koe de yobareta!
Shukkoo suru toki ni
  sasu no umeki wa arimasen yoo ni,

demo nemutte iru no yoo ni ugoite shio,
  oto to awa no tame tsuyosugiru,
mugen no suishin kara totta no wa
  kaeru toki ni.

Tasogaredoki to yuugata no yobirin
  sore kara kurayami da!
Fune ni noru toki ni
  wakare wa kanashiku de wa nai yoo ni;

tabun shio wa kono jidai to basho kara
  watashi o tooku e hakobu keredo,
sasu o wattata no ato de mizusaki annainin o
  chokusetsu au koto ga dekitai.

1889

Questions for discussion

1. What is the capital of Indonesia? What are the country's main exports? Do drivers in Indonesia drive on the right, as we do, or on the left?
2. Where is the Hermitage? Who used to live there? Why do you think it is called "The Hermitage"?
3. What happens at a Japanese wedding? True or False: People in Japan are mostly Christians. Why do foreign countries have different religions?
4. What happened in Hong Kong on July 1st, 1997? Why did it happen? Explain.
5. What is a popular pastime in the city of Macau? List three reasons why this pastime is harmful.
6. What are the two official languages of Canada? Why do you suppose the people of Quebec might want independence? How would that affect our country? Discuss.
7. What are two different meanings of the word "device"? Do you think that devices are useful? What devices do you use in your own life?
8. Do you think this book is an autobiography? Why or why not? Which do you like better, true stories or fiction? Why?
9. What did you like about this book? What did you not like? Discuss.
10. Have you ever had an experience in which something turned out to be not what you thought it was or not what you expected? What happened? How did you feel?

```
10 LET A$="Moko and Now, after the bubble"; LET A=12
20 LET B$="Simultaneous Brazil"; LET B=5
30 LET C$="Morphology of the Hermitage by Vladimir Propp"; LET C=12
40 LET D$="On opening the door of my mind, I could..."; LET D=2
50 LET E$="Something other than patacas"; LET E=11
60 LET F$="1996 Rehabilitated"; LET F=28
70 LET G$="Tom & Jerry, on the ferry"; LET G=3
80 LET H$="Gulliver's Travels"; LET H=8
90 LET I$="A small complicated underground city"; LET I=17
100 LET J$="Blood and gasoline"; LET J=8
110 LET K$="Michel Rivard would like to see the sea"; LET K=10
120 LET L$="Being, with Americans"; LET L=4
130 LET M$="Left to my own devices"; LET M=11
140 LET P=17
150 PRINT "Table of Contents"
155 PRINT A$;P
160 PRINT B$;P+A
165 PRINT C$;P+A+B+1
170 PRINT D$;P+A+B+C
175 PRINT E$;P+A+B+C+D
180 PRINT F$;P+A+B+C+D+E+1
185 PRINT G$;P+A+B+C+D+E+F
190 PRINT H$;P+A+B+C+D+E+F+G+3
195 PRINT I$;P+A+B+C+D+E+F+G+H
200 PRINT J$;P+A+B+C+D+E+F+G+H+I+1
205 PRINT K$;P+A+B+C+D+E+F+G+H+I+J
210 PRINT L$;P+A+B+C+D+E+F+G+H+I+J+K
215 PRINT M$;P+A+B+C+D+E+F+G+H+I+J+K+L+2
220 INPUT "WOULD YOU LIKE TO SEE THE SEA?";Z$
230 IF Z$="YES" THEN 250
240 GOTO 150
250 END

RUN

Table of Contents
Moko and Now, after the bubble 17
Simultaneous Brazil 29
Morphology of the Hermitage by Vladimir Propp 35
On opening the door of my mind, I could... 47
Something other than patacas 49
1996 Rehabilitated 61
Tom & Jerry, on the ferry 89
Gulliver's Travels 95
A small complicated underground city 103
Blood and gasoline 121
Michel Rivard would like to see the sea 129
Being, with Americans 139
Left to my own devices 145
WOULD YOU LIKE TO SEE THE SEA?_
```

machine
Television
Book
Megaphone
(Fog machine)
Ferry
Web-page
BLOOD
Kerosene
Heater
Typewriter
Propellor
Microphone
Pager
Toilet
0
1500 feet
0
500 meters
Doorbell
Voicemail
MD Player / Earphones
Honda
Shin-Kobe Tunnel
CD Player
6
KOTATSU TABLE-
CALCULATOR
Electric Guitar
Metronome
Email
ANSWERING
MACHINE
E
Robot
MP3 / Subway
VCR
DNA
IV
Record Player
J
Z
Computer
Golden peacock
Map
1
9
CAMERA-CELLPHONE
KEY
VIDEO
RADIO
Names
Money
Chindogu
Light-
Emitting
Diode

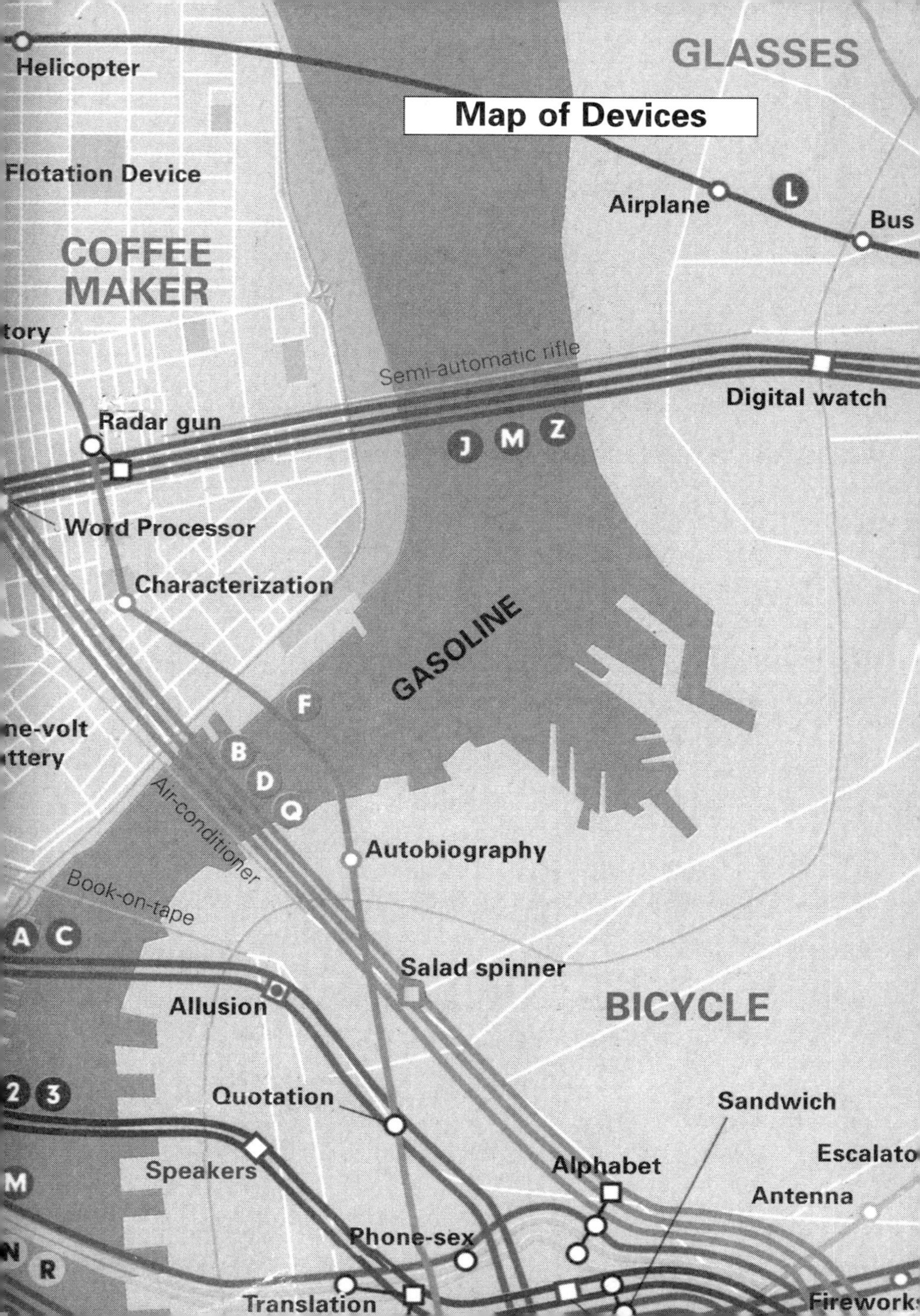
Map of Devices
Helicopter
GLASSES
Flotation Device
Airplane
L
Bus
COFFEE
MAKER
tory
Semi-automatic rifle
Digital watch
Radar gun
J
M
Z
Word Processor
Characterization
GASOLINE
F
ne-volt
ttery
B
D
Q
Air-conditioner
Autobiography
Book-on-tape
A
C
Salad spinner
Allusion
BICYCLE
2
3
Quotation
Sandwich
Speakers
Alphabet
Escalato
M
Antenna
Phone-sex
N
R
Translation
Fireworks

The author was born on January 22, 1972, in Summerside, Prince Edward Island. The death of the author was declared by Roland Barthes four years previous to this. According to conventional wisdom, first books are always autobiographical. Second books appropriate the narratives of other, more vulnerable selves. Those authors who do not have access to a narrative of a unified self will be required by the exigencies of this convention to invent one. This is my first book. An author can not be considered to have "found his voice" until he has published at least two books with a recognized publisher. Corey Haim divides his time between Toronto and Los Angeles. Write to: Corey Haim, c/o King Talent, #303-228 E. 4th Avenue, Vancouver, BC, Canada V5T-1G5.